"You didn't know t[...] was a serial killer?

The judgment was there in Mitch's eyes, the same as she'd seen in the courtroom, from the cops, from the people who drove by her house and threw rocks through her windows, flattened her tires, sent death threats.

Jane swallowed hard against an onslaught of bitter tears. "I was blind, stupid blind, but I did not know."

A long moment passed between them. "You're right. I don't believe you."

She sagged. What else had she expected? "Okay. Don't believe me, but Wade has come here to kill you and after he does that, he'll kill me, too."

"Why would he want to kill you? If you're really innocent, why would Wade want to do that?"

"Because he will eventually find out that I have something he wants, something that I won't ever give to him while I have breath in my body."

"What could you have that would make him care enough to come after you?"

Her head spun and she fought for breath.

"I have his son."

Dana Mentink is a national bestselling author. She has been honored to win two Carol Awards, a HOLT Medallion and an RT Reviewers' Choice Best Book Award. She's authored more than thirty novels to date for Love Inspired Suspense and Harlequin Heartwarming. Dana loves feedback from her readers. Contact her at danamentink.com.

Visit the Author Profile page at Harlequin.com for more titles.

Danger on the Ranch

Dana Mentink

HARLEQUIN® LOVE INSPIRED® SUSPENSE

Recycling programs for this product may not exist in your area.

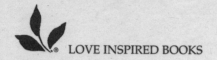 LOVE INSPIRED BOOKS

ISBN-13: 978-1-335-23216-8

Danger on the Ranch

www.Harlequin.com

Printed in U.S.A.

For I am persuaded, that neither death,
nor life, nor angels, nor principalities,
nor powers, nor things present, nor things to come,

Nor height, nor depth, nor any other creature,
shall be able to separate us from the love of God,
which is in Christ Jesus our Lord.
–*Romans* 8:38-39

To Ann P., my golden-hearted friend.

ONE

Storm's coming.

The illogical notion trickled again through Mitch Whitehorse's gut as he surveyed the late-afternoon fog choking the windswept cove. Strange, since there was no sign of a weather front moving in through the mist. He fingered the scar that grooved his cheek, the rough patch oddly numb, a dead spot courtesy of his brother. The occasional blurred vision and migraines were an additional reminder of how close he'd come to dying at Wade's hand.

But it wasn't so much the pain of having his occipital bone crushed or the resulting symptoms that stuck in his mind—it was his brother's smile. Even when Wade was led from the courtroom after the guilty verdict that would send him to prison for life, he'd been smiling right at Mitch, a smile of pure evil, cold as the grave, unrepentant, undefeated.

Rosie, the big roan mare, shifted underneath Mitch, probably wondering why they were standing on a bluff in the numbing fog, staring out at the crawling Pacific instead of sheltering from the February wind. They'd spent a full day moving a herd of cattle from one pasture to another and chasing down an ailing cow to administer medicine. Straightening, Mitch ignored the twinge in his back, courtesy of his days as a US marshal and the fact that he was now a hardworking cowboy staring forty in the face.

Storm's coming.

There it was again, the warning his instincts kept whispering in spite of what his eyes could see.

Pure silliness. Nothing could shake Mitch anymore, least of all a mere storm. The worst evil he'd ever encountered, Wade's heinous killing spree that left three women dead, was over. Wade was in prison, Mitch's final act as a US marshal before he'd walked away from law enforcement and onto his uncle Gus's Roughwater Ranch. He hadn't put Wade's wife, Jane Reyes, away for life, like he should have. Jane knew all too well that Wade had abducted those women, imprisoned them right on their sprawling property, killed them one by one, except for the last. Oh, he knew she had been an accomplice, but knowing and proving were two different things. Her sentence would have to come later.

Someone else's battle to fight.

He eased the horse into motion. They took the trail down to the beach. Just a short ride to clear his head before they made their way back to his cabin tucked in the grove of trees far away from any living creature except his two horses. He had two, because living things weren't meant to go it alone, except for Mitch Whitehorse. That was why he didn't live on the ranch property like the other hands. It was one of the reasons, anyway.

Down where the salt water scoured the beach, he noticed right away the rough gouge of sand where a boat had been dragged up onto the shore by a trespasser. No sign of the boat now.

Habit had him reaching for the sidearm that was no longer there, hadn't been for two years. It was just a boat, he told himself as he dismounted and left Rosie to nose at the clumps of seagrass. Though the beach was property of the ranch, Uncle Gus didn't mind the odd fisherman or adventuring honeymooners looking for their own quiet stretch of sand.

But this section of beach was rocky, cold, perpetually blasted by wind, with no calm water to attract fish or people. His cabin was tucked behind the cliff close by, too close, and Mitch did not like people anywhere in the vicinity.

A clump of rocks rose in an untidy pile on the edge of the sand crescent before it was cut off by the cliffs. Big enough to hide a boat. He approached at an angle— old cop habit. There would be nothing to find but some harmless guy, taking time out to smoke a cigarette, or a beachcomber hunting for shells. The central California coast, after all, was a place that encouraged solitude, and that was why it was perfect for Mitch.

But the clenched muscles in his gut refused to relax as he reached the rock pile, skirted it and found the boat. It was a plain aluminum vessel with an outboard motor, glinting in the sunlight. Probably a rental from the dive shop. No one around.

If Mitch was a normal guy, he'd have his cell phone out, taking pictures, calling the local cops to report a trespasser, but he carried no cell phone and never intended to again. He waited, listening over the sound of the waves for the intruder's whereabouts. Nothing. The wind whipped his battered cowboy hat, threatening to snatch it, as he hunkered down. Nothing and no one, not for the ten minutes he waited there.

Rosie nickered from the far end of the beach, her way of saying, "Whatsa matter with you?"

Good question. He turned to go.

A figure rose up from the rocks above, backlit by the fog-dulled sun. Black ski cap pulled down across the brow, wiry torso covered by a nylon windbreaker, black jeans, booted feet. Mitch could not see clearly for a moment, but he did not need to. His senses could not believe it was his brother, Wade, standing on the rocks staring down, but his heart told him it could be no one else.

Wade cracked a smile. "Hello, big brother. You're ugly as ever. Scar hasn't faded, has it?"

The ripped edges of the wound had healed, but the real damage never would. His brother, his blood kin, the psychopath, had escaped from prison. Mitch's worst fear stood above him like the creatures from the old monster movies he'd watched as a kid. He'd stopped watching those flicks when he'd learned that man was the greatest monster of all, this man in particular, his brother, Wade.

Wade's left hand was concealed behind his back. Mitch knew what was coming. Wade had him pinned right and proper. Wade was smart, probably smarter than Mitch. Only Mitch's dogged determination had brought him down, but now Wade had the upper hand in every way.

You're an idiot, Mitch, he told himself. Aloud he said, "Finished that prison sentence already?"

Wade laughed. "You know I'm the impatient type. Remember when I took your horse because Mom wouldn't let me have the car?"

He remembered. Wade had whipped the horse until

its sides were bloody, and Mitch had been so furious it had ended in a fistfight, with Pops barely able to separate them. It always ended badly when he was anywhere near his brother. The darkness in Wade's soul rubbed off on those around him, like he suspected it had on Wade's wife, Jane. Then again, maybe she'd been just as twisted as him from the get-go. Venomous, that was Wade Whitehorse, and anyone who stayed around him long enough got a full dose.

"Prison didn't agree with me." Wade smiled, teeth glaring white in the sunlight. "And I had a few debts to settle up, of course."

"So you borrowed a boat and came to find me. I'm flattered."

"You're sloppy, and the boat isn't mine. I don't like the water, you remember. I prefer horseback. You have a routine, exercising your horse here along the beach at just this hour. You made it easy. Easier than escaping from the marshals during the prison transfer." He clucked. "Disappointing."

Now the hand came around from behind and Mitch saw the gun. He knew it instantly, bile rising in his throat.

Wade smiled. "You recognize it, I can tell."

"Granddad's revolver." Passed down to their father. The first time he'd ever fired a gun had been with that revolver, his father standing tall and proud behind him. He'd loved that gun. "Wondered where it got to."

"Pops never let me have it. I hated him for that."

"He didn't want to give a gun to a psychopath." Mitch shrugged. "It's called good parenting."

Wade's eyes narrowed for a moment, and Mitch braced for impact. Instead Wade laughed. "It's okay. I got what

I wanted. Stole it out of Pops's gun safe when I was sixteen."

"So how do you happen to have it now? Didn't think they let psychos bring their guns to jail."

"My wife stored it away for me. Janey. You remember Janey?"

He didn't answer.

"She's a good wifey, that Janey, in most ways."

Wade's fixed stare flickered a moment, caught by some movement Mitch couldn't see on the water's edge under the rotted dock pilings. His horse? Wade trained the gun away from him.

"Don't you shoot that horse," Mitch snapped.

Wade turned back, smiled. "I didn't come here to shoot the horse." Wade fired as Mitch surged forward in a futile effort. He felt a crease of heat on his temple and then he was falling into darkness. Just before the black closed in, he noticed a plume of smoke arcing over the sand like a striking snake.

She'd been too late. Mitch collapsed to the sand. Berating herself, Jane Reyes fired a second flare, aiming directly for Wade's chest. She didn't know if a flare would kill a person, but it might knock him back enough to warn him off. The horse waiting far off on the beach sprang into a gallop, ears pinned.

A shot whistled over her head, and she ducked down behind the dock pilings that hid her. They were remnants of some rudimentary boat landing that had long ago given way to the sea. Her breath came in panicked gasps as she crouched there. Would he come after her? She had no more flares and only a knife tucked into her boot. She'd been trying to pick out the rugged path up to Mitch's property, after beaching her rented boat on the shore. Wind plucked at her hair, numbed her limbs.

Now she was trapped here, no cell reception, Mitch shot and probably bleeding to death, and her ex-husband stalking her from a scant fifty yards away from his perch on the rock pile. There was no one to help. Again she questioned the sanity of a man who lived in a location with limited access, by horseback, boat or on foot. So lonely, so desolate.

And why had *she* come here to this isolated stretch of nowhere to find Mitch? Put herself in such a vulnerable position for a man who believed she was a willing participant in Wade's sick plans?

Because Wade was her worst nightmare, evil incarnate, and he'd found the house where she rented a tiny back room from Nana Jo. It was only by God's grace that she'd been out at the time, able to flee. Mitch White-horse was the only one…the only person on earth who could help her put Wade back in prison, where he could not destroy any more lives. Only now Mitch was likely dead. Icy despair licked at her.

You can't give up.

Wade's voice, singsong and high-pitched, carried over the wind. "Who's that shooting at me?"

Terror coursed through her at the sound of that voice, and his courtroom promise returned to her mind.

We'll be together again, Janey. Don't you worry, my dove. The smile, the soulless eyes. *I'll never let you go.*

She clamped her teeth closed to hold in the scream and clutched the useless flare gun. Where was he? Still at a distance, judging from the voice. Stopped to examine her boat? Circling around to her position? She could not see through the thickening fog.

A flicker of movement up and to the right riveted her. He was climbing to a higher position, a spot on top of the craggy pile from which he'd be able to pick out her hiding place. But his movement gave her time, minutes maybe, no longer, while he threaded his way along the rocks. If she could reach Mitch, the boat, and get them into the water... The little outboard motor wasn't terribly powerful and she'd be fighting the incoming tide, but it would put some distance between them, and maybe she could make it past the cove, out of range of Wade's gun.

One thing she knew after a year of marriage to the monster was that Wade Whitehorse could not swim. Forcing herself to breathe slowly, she counted to three, pushed off from the rotted piling and ran as quietly as she could. Every moment she expected the report of a gun, the pain of a bullet plowing into her skull.

Panting, fueled by terror, she made it to Mitch and the boat.

As frightened as she was of Wade, it scared her even more to crouch behind a pile of sand next to Mitch's sprawled body. He lay on his back, face turned toward her, one muscled arm out-flung. Blood stained his forehead, collecting in the puckered edges of his scar, dripping down to saturate the collar of his barn jacket. With shaking fingers, she checked for a pulse. His dark lashes twitched as she touched his cold throat.

Alive.

Mitch Whitehorse was alive.

A rock bounced loose from the towering cliff and tumbled to the beach. Wade was closing in, and if she didn't do something fast, neither one of them would live to see morning.

TWO

Mitch's senses came back online slowly, feeding him bits of information that did not make sense. Pain, in his temple and back. Cold, the feel of wind on his face and damp sand under his body. Fear, that he was being dragged against his will to a place he did not want to go. He forced his eyes open. Someone was yanking him by the arm, trying to heave him up and into the aluminum boat he'd noticed just before Wade shot him.

Wade.

Mitch surged to his feet in an adrenaline-fueled rush, pulling free of his captor before he toppled backward into the sand. A woman with long dark hair swooped next him. It took him a few blinks to recognize her, Jane Reyes Whitehorse, his brother's wife.

"Don't touch me." He tried to get up again, but his head spun. She grabbed a handful of his shirtfront with one hand and clamped icy fingers over his mouth with the other.

"Be quiet. He'll hear you. You've got to get in the boat. Help me. I can't move you by myself."

He shook off her grasp.

"I don't know what you're trying to do…" he grated out.

"Save your life, you big ox, and if you don't help me right now, Wade is going to kill us both."

Both? Kill his accomplice? Mitch shook himself to try to clear away the fuzz, but the movement made him groan. She was grabbing him again, yanking and pulling, and he moved more to get her to stop jarring his nerves into white-hot pain than to cooperate. Suddenly he found himself in the bottom of the boat that she began to drag to the water's edge.

He clamped a palm over the gunwale and hauled himself up to his knees, but she'd managed to get the boat in the water and it was all he could do to hold on against the movement.

There was a crack, the whistling noise that he didn't have to see to know was a bullet. She threw herself to her knees.

"Wade?" he grunted.

"Who else?"

"Why's he shooting at you?"

Her eyes rounded in exasperation. "He's shooting at you. I don't think he knows it's me yet. You didn't know he'd escaped from the marshals?"

"Just found that out." Before he'd formulated his next question, she yanked the outboard to life. The motor throbbed, and she guided the boat into the grip of the tide. He would rather have jumped into the waves and swum than been in the company of his former sister-in-law and the woman who'd aided Wade in his horrors, but his vision was blurred and there was a dull ringing in his ears. He forced himself to breathe through his nose, praying the dizziness would subside long enough for him to take action. Another bullet followed the first, closer this time. Wade had gotten to a better position for the kill shot.

Now he'd hauled himself to his knees just as a shot took a chunk out of the side of the boat, startling Jane. She flipped over backward into the waves, going under. Breaking the surface a moment later, she looked at him with wide eyes of a color caught between ice blue and silver. She coughed, wet hair clinging in long dark clumps to her cheeks.

Indecision clawed at him. She was his enemy, but she was also a woman, a small woman with a mouth pinched in fear. Without allowing himself to think it over, he stuck an oar over the side, and she grabbed on.

Fighting through pain and the disequilibrium of the rocking boat, he began to pull her in, until another shot furrowed the water so close she lost her grip. Hands flailing, she fought against the current, but it sucked her back toward the rocks. He tumbled out after her, a messy splash into cold that seeped right into his core.

He struck out as best he could in the direction she'd been swept. Without the protection of the boat, there would be nothing stopping Wade from shooting them except perhaps the layer of fog, which had thickened to be almost impenetrable.

His fingers felt something soft, and he grabbed at it. It turned out to be her jacket sleeve. He clung to her wrist and reeled the rest of her body close to his until he'd encircled her in his arms. She was smaller than he'd thought.

She looked up at him with those strange-colored eyes.

The lights from a boat sliced through the water, bouncing off the mist. "Driftwood Police Department," a voice called. "This is private property, and there is no shooting allowed here." It was a voice Mitch knew well. Danny Patron, an avid fisherman, hardworking cop and father of three, who was assigned the lonely job of watching the coastline.

"Hey," he yelled. "Danny! Over here." He continued to shout as loud as he could, and Jane joined him, but the thrum of the motor indicated the vessel was passing them, unaware of the two victims fighting the waves and buried in fog.

By now Mitch was tiring, the energy seeping out of him as he struggled to tread water. He could not see what had become of the boat, and it took all his reserves to keep them from smashing against the sharp rocks.

He realized Jane had freed herself from his grasp and taken hold of his sleeve. He resisted, but she dug her fingers into his bicep.

"This way."

Again, he was forced to make a decision—follow a woman he would not even trust with his cowboy boots, or stay put, fighting the tide until he would certainly drown?

"Where…?" he tried, but she did not allow him to utter the rest. He found himself towed along through the icy water, following the woman who'd married the monster.

Jane felt as though her limbs were carved from a block of ice. She held on to Mitch as long as she could, but he slipped out of her numb grasp at some point, though she could still see his dark head just behind. He shouted a couple of times, but she could not understand over the roar of the surf, nor did she want to.

There was only one thing on her mind: getting them out of the freezing grip of the waves before they drowned.

Her knee banged into a submerged ridge, the bottom of the cliff that rose straight from the water like a shark fin. She hauled herself out, gasping as the wind robbed her of any remaining warmth.

"What do you think you're doing?" Mitch grunted behind her. "If you climb, he's got an easy target."

She didn't respond, fingers clawing as the rocks tore into her flesh. It was here, had to be.

"Hey," he said, but his words were cut off by a grunt of pain. From his injury or the rocks that surely sliced at him, too.

What if she'd been wrong? Again? What if Mitch was right and there was nothing on this cliff but certain death? No, this would not be the end. This was her only shot at life, real life, one last chance to make things right. Teeth gritted, she hauled herself along the sharp crack, praying that the fog and the police had been enough to frighten Wade away.

But Wade was never scared.

That part of him was missing; instead there was an empty void where human feeling should reside.

She was shivering uncontrollably now. Her legs felt like they were as insubstantial as the fog. Despair gripped its way into her belly. And then she saw it, the cutout that marked the cave she'd spotted on her way into the cove, high enough that the tide would not flood it, or so she hoped.

"Come on," she ordered him and climbed as quickly as she could until she crawled through the opening. It was a harder squeeze for Mitch, as the guy was broad shouldered and a hulk at somewhere over six feet.

He hunched inside the cave, water streaming from his clothing, eyes ink dark, narrow, suspicious.

"You're Wade's wife."

It was like the executioner pronouncing sentence.

"No. Divorced."

"Why are you here?" His shirt was stained with blood, and his teeth were chattering as badly as hers.

"Sit down," she said.

"I don't take orders from you."

"Okay then, stand, but when you fall over, try not to hit your head. You probably already have a concussion."

He did not sit, but she noticed he grabbed an outcropping of rock with one massive palm.

She scanned the cave floor until she found a meager supply of semidry leaves and some driftwood. Piling it onto the driest spot she could find, she pulled the Ziploc bag from her jacket pocket. With trembling fingers, she struck the match. It fizzled as soon as she touched it to the leaves.

"We won't have to worry that he'll see the smoke with all this fog," she said, more to herself than him. *I hope.* There wasn't much choice, anyway. They were dangerously close to hypothermia. Cold or bullets? Which one would get them first? She ground her teeth together. Neither, if she had a teaspoon of strength left in her. Patting her pockets, she realized her cell phone was somewhere at the bottom of the cove. At least the small pouch hooked to her belt was still there, for what it was worth. Her driver's license, ATM card and a soggy ten-dollar bill. Not much, but keeping hold of some small thing helped her feel the tiniest bit less exposed.

Mitch swabbed a sleeve over his face. "Where'd you get the matches?"

"There was a kit in the boat. I grabbed it just before I started the motor. I thought there might be some first-aid supplies."

He was silent as she struck the second match, which was snuffed just as quickly.

"Here," he said, dropping to one knee and taking the box of matches from her. He bent close to the debris with a wince and a groan. Slowly, patiently, he held the lit match to the barest edge of the driest clump of pine needles. It kindled orange and smoked. He blew softly, cupping his shaking hand around the needles until they were fully aflame. With more gentleness than she'd thought him capable of, he eased the pine needles back into the pile. She held her breath as the debris grudgingly took.

Fighting back tears of relief, she scooted as close as she could to that small spot of warmth. With quaking fingers, she fished out a bandage from the bag and thrust it at him. "You're still bleeding."

Ignoring her offering, Mitch eased to a sitting position across from her, mouth tight with pain. "Why are you here?"

"To find you. And it wasn't easy. You have no cell phone, and your house is like some kind of remote fortress or something."

"Not remote enough, if you found it."

She pushed another twig into the fire and edged so close her knees were almost touching the flames. "I… came to warn you that Wade had escaped."

"Police could tell me that. So why did you come? Not just to warn me. You don't care about me. Why?"

She was quiet. The little flames danced and popped, painting light and darkness across his face. Was there any of Wade's darkness in his brother, Mitch? They shared genes.

That doesn't mean anything, she told herself savagely. *DNA doesn't determine who you are—your soul does.* But what kind of soul did Mitch Whitehorse have? Didn't matter. He was the one, the only one, who could save what mattered most.

"I came because I need you to help me put Wade back in prison."

He blinked. "So now you're afraid of him, too? Why? You turned a blind eye while he kidnapped and murdered three women."

She sucked in a breath. "I know you don't believe me, but I didn't know what Wade was doing."

"You didn't know the guy you married was a serial killer?"

The judgment was there in his eyes, the same she'd seen in the courtroom, the cops, the people who drove by her house and threw rocks into her windows, flattened her tires, sent death threats.

She swallowed hard against an onslaught of bitter tears. "I was blind, stupid blind, but I did not know."

A long moment passed between them. "You're right. I don't believe you."

She sagged. What else had she expected? Why would Mitch be any different? "Okay. Don't believe me, but Wade has come here to kill you, and after he does that, he'll kill me, too."

"Why would he want to kill you? If you're really innocent, why would Wade want to do that?"

"Because he will eventually find out that I have something he wants, something that I won't ever give to him while I have breath in my body."

"What could you have that would make him care enough to come after you?"

Her head spun, and she fought for breath. Tell him? What choice did she have?

"I have his son."

THREE

She was lying, Mitch thought. Manipulating him, just like Wade. He crawled to the cave entrance both to scan for any sign of Wade or the returning police and to give himself a moment to think. It wasn't easy with the hammering pain inside his skull and the cold that still made every movement arduous.

I have his son.

"I was pregnant," she said, so low he almost didn't hear it. "At the time…when things began to come out. I…I didn't love Wade, hadn't for a long time, when I began to notice things about him, scary things." Her gulped breath made something inside him tense. "I was making secret plans to get away, which I'm sure you don't believe." Flames crackled as she threw another twig on the fire. "I was only four weeks along when the police came to arrest Wade. Two months at the time of the trial."

"And he didn't know?"

"No, but I was terrified he'd guess. I moved away and changed my identity. Wade found my hiding place two days ago, but I was out at the time and I got away."

"Why'd he come for you, then, if you aren't his accomplice?"

He saw a shudder pass through her. "He told me we'd always be together. I think he believes I belong to him and I'd help him."

The starkness in her tone was convincing, but he'd heard a lot of convincing liars before. "Where's the kid?"

She flinched. "Somewhere close. Safe."

He yanked around to look at her. "Where?"

Her eyes flashed silver fire at him. "Somewhere safe," she repeated, the words hard and clipped. Then she cleared her throat. "Ben is not even three yet, so he doesn't understand any of this."

"You need to tell me where he is."

Her chin went up. "I don't need to tell you anything."

He stepped closer, staring her down. "If Wade suspects, he'll get to your boy, no matter what kind of hiding place you've found."

Her chin trembled, or maybe it was a trick of the firelight. "You don't think I know that?"

"Then tell the cops. They'll protect you."

Her laugh was filled with bitterness. "The cops didn't keep Wade in prison. They didn't prevent people from sending me death threats and vandalizing my house. No one protected me."

"Because you and your husband killed three women and almost a fourth if she hadn't gotten away."

She jerked as if he'd slapped her, then wrapped her arms around her middle and stared at him. "I…didn't… know." The lines around her mouth were hard, and every muscle in her frame was taut. "I didn't know." She moved quickly, snatched up a stick and cracked it in two. "You'll never believe me. Think what you want, but…" Her voice broke. She cleared her throat and re-started. "My son, my little boy, does not deserve to pay the price for his father's crimes. Please." She was still on her knees, crouched in front of the meager fire. "Please help me. I have no one else."

No one else.

He rubbed a hand through his hair, but it ignited a trail of pain, so he stopped. "I'm not your guy."

"I saved your life."

"I didn't ask you to." His harsh tone bounced back to him.

She stood now. "I'm not asking for myself. This isn't about my life. It's about my son's."

Silence grew between them, interrupted only by the pop and hiss of the fire.

"Right now we have to figure out how to get out of this cave without getting shot. That's all." He turned his back on her again and surveyed the cove. The fog had thinned a bit after the sun sank into the choppy waters. It was almost fully dark. The only way they were going to survive was to retreat from the cave back up to the trail that loped along the cliff top.

"Gonna climb up to the trail. Rosie will get us back to my place."

"Who's Rosie?"

"My horse."

"I saw her run away."

"She's somewhere, waiting for my signal."

"How do you know?"

He didn't answer. "You can warm up and I'll give you some clothes. I'll take you to the police when it's safe."

"So you won't help me yourself?"

He tossed another twig into the fire. "We'll leave it burning. If Wade is watching, might be a diversion."

"Do you think Wade's given up by now?"

"Do you?"

Her gaze became uncertain, dropped away. "No." She paused. "Soon after we were married, a couple of teenage boys snuck onto our property and had a little party. They didn't damage anything, just left some bottles and a bag from their snacks. Wade hid there every night for five weeks until they came back, and then he scared them so badly they never returned." She shivered, and he suspected it wasn't from the cold. "Every single night for five weeks."

She knew just as well as he.

Wade hadn't given up, and he never would. Their best and only chance was to use darkness to conceal their escape.

But Wade knew how to use the darkness, too.

Like the monster hiding in the shadows, waiting for the kill.

They crawled out of the cave, and every inch of Jane's body screamed in protest. Cold air whipped her mercilessly and she felt powerless against the elements, to the threat that was waiting out there. Mitch startled her by gripping her shoulder. His hands were massive, but his touch was surprisingly light.

"Stay low. Keep a couple of feet back from me so you have time to get away if he starts shooting."

And what was she supposed to do if Mitch got shot again? She decided to keep that thought to herself. *One foot in front of the other, Jane.* It took her feet and her clawed fingers to cling to the slippery rocks. Mitch tried to keep them in cover as best he could, and she hoped the fog was enough to conceal them further. Still, her skin prickled both from the cold and the knowledge that Wade was out there.

Did he know it was her?

Who's that shooting at me?

He probably did not blame her for her testimony—she had in fact known nothing about his crimes—but the divorce papers he'd been served in prison had been another matter. He'd never signed, and she'd had to withstand the interminable statutory waiting period before the marriage was dissolved without his consent.

I'll never let you go.

She thought for the millionth time about what kind of a man he'd seemed to be, charming, sweet, thoughtful, intelligent. And he'd used those charms to lure young women, abduct them and force them to deplete their bank accounts. Then he'd imprisoned each for some sick, twisted thrill only he understood before he killed them. How had she not known? Not seen? Not heard anything from the underground bunker in the woods where he'd kept them chained?

And why hadn't he done the same to her?

As soon as he discovered she'd gone to his brother, he'd come after her with the full force of his evil. And if somehow he found out about Ben… The thought made her move quicker, edging closer to Mitch as they climbed up the cliff side.

When she thought she could stand no more, when her palms were shredded and her muscles aching, they made it over the top. They lay panting in a grassy field, peppered with clumps of trees and scrubby bushes.

Mitch got to his feet first, put his fingers to his lips and whistled. It barely carried over the sound of the wind. She struggled to her feet and looked for any sign of Mitch's horse. Seconds ticked into minutes.

"Which way is your place?" She found she had to bend over to continue sucking in deep lungfuls of air. "We'll have to hike."

The ground vibrated under her feet, and a big mare trotted up, reins trailing.

For the first time, she saw Mitch Whitehorse smile. He ran his hands over the animal's sides. "You were scared, weren't you, Rosie girl? It's okay now. I'm here."

What tender words from a man who had about as much give as granite. Nonetheless, she was so happy to see that horse show up, she might have kissed both of them on the spot.

He leaned his forehead against the horse's neck and she thought at first it was a sign of affection, until she realized Mitch looked unsteady on his feet.

"Are you okay?"

He straightened. "Yeah." But as he heaved himself onto the horse, he had to grip the saddle hard, face pale in the moonlight. He bent and extended his palm. "Climb up."

"Uh…" It was not the time to tell him she knew precisely nothing about riding. As she clutched his forearm, he swung her so she landed just behind the saddle. "Hold on to the cantle and keep your feet away from her flanks."

She had no idea what either "cantle" or "flanks" meant, but she tucked up her legs and grabbed on to the leather seat back where Mitch sat. There was no way she would wrap her arms around him, that was for sure.

She wondered if the horse had the strength to carry

both of them after wandering loose for hours, but Rosie seemed to respond quickly to Mitch's click of the tongue.

"How far?"

"What?" he called over his shoulder.

"I said, 'How far?'" she started to shout when a gunshot broke the night. Jane felt the movement of air as the shot went past, and then the horse was running full out.

She grabbed Mitch around the waist to keep from falling, and they galloped into the trees. Was Wade on foot? Horseback? On a motorcycle? She didn't hear an engine, but the sound of her own frightened breathing and the pounding of the horse's hooves would probably have drowned it out anyway.

Rosie kept to the trees, slowing only enough to dodge branches and piles of rocks. No more bullets followed. Rosie slackened her pace. The woods fell into silence, broken only by the creak of the leather saddle and Rosie's soft whinny. Jane began to believe, to hope, that Wade had not followed them into the woods, until his voice carried over the night noise.

"Hey, Mitch. Who's that with you? Have you got yourself a girl?" Wade asked in that singsong way that prickled her skin. Then his tone went hard and lethal.

"Or have you taken mine?"

FOUR

The high trill of Wade's voice brought back all the horror in one flash of skin-rippling nausea. Though Mitch had desperately wanted to deny the accusations against his brother, he'd known deep down that every terrible detail was true. Wade Whitehorse was a psychopath, capable of unspeakable evil.

In spite of the respite he'd found working at Uncle Gus's Roughwater Ranch, part of him had always known this day might come, the day his brother returned to destroy him.

Mitch could feel Jane's hands clutching the back of his shirt. Terror, it could not be anything else. So now she was scared of him? After being married to Wade and turning a blind eye to his brutal treatment of other women? It was incomprehensible. He bit back the rage and urged Rosie deeper into the woods.

"Where is he?" Jane hissed.

"At our ten o'clock, on foot, unless he's got a horse."

"We have to get out of these woods." Her panic transmitted clearly as she grabbed his waist and pressed her cheek to his back. "Please."

Please. An odd word for a killer's wife to choose. He

pressed Rosie to go deeper into the screen of trees. The branches shuttered out the moonlight, leaving them in inky gloom. Now her breathing was coming in frightened pants.

"He'll find us here—he probably has tools, night-vision goggles, military equipment."

I know, he wanted to snap at her. *Tools he used to imprison women while you stayed quiet and let him.* He clucked to Rosie encouragingly, urging her around a fallen oak, squeezing between clefts of rocks into what looked like a wild tangle of overgrowth.

He could not see, so instead he let himself feel, turning his face until he caught the whiff of air that smelled of wet granite, cooled as it swept down from the mountain. He turned the horse east.

Jane clutched him tighter. "There's no path. We can't hide. He'll find us."

He'll find us. Mitch had felt this showdown would come since that moment he'd seen his brother smile as he was taken to prison, but it could not happen now, not when Mitch was dizzy and weak, with Jane clinging to his back.

"What are you doing?" she whispered.

He didn't answer, merely guided Rosie along, following the trail of chilled air. The ground was moist, muddy in some places, which caused the horse to slow. Mitch smiled. The more mud, the better. They had to push through dense thickets, which proved no trouble for Rosie, though the branches scratched at him and probably Jane a few times. The thicker the screen, the deeper the layer of muck under Rosie's hooves, the better he felt. If Wade was on horseback, there was a slim chance he could follow their trail in the darkness, but if he was on foot, he would wait until daylight. One thing he knew about his brother—Wade could not stand to be dirty, not even for one moment.

He recalled his own laughter as a high school senior when he and his girlfriend Paige Lynn came upon Wade, staring at the brown smear on his palm from the front door they'd just painted at their parents' dilapidated house in Arizona. They'd offered Wade a rag, but he'd been so enraged he'd thrown it back at them, along with a vile diatribe that brought the neighbors outside. Wade had finally composed himself, and Mitch and Paige Lynn repainted the marred spot on the door. The next day Mitch found the front windshield of his car smashed, the interior ruined with paint.

A thorn scratched his arm, but he hardly felt it through the cold. Pushing through a heavily forested area over the mucky ground would not be an option for Wade and might be the only thing that kept them alive.

Jane had given up trying to question him, finally, which was a relief since they were both shivering fit to beat the band. He tried to blink away the waves of dizziness that hit him. If he fell from the horse…

Grasping the reins tighter, he stiffened his spine. Only another quarter mile, he figured. At one point he stopped Rosie.

Jane clutched at him. "What? Did you hear him? Has he found us?"

"Quiet," he commanded.

Surprisingly, she obeyed.

He heard nothing but the branches rattling in the wind like the sound of dried bones. A light rain had begun to fall. Her fingers were dead cold on his back. If they did not get to his cabin soon, they would both fall victim to hypothermia.

Rosie responded eagerly to his click of the tongue and picked up her pace. Again they passed through an area of dense foliage, and he heard Jane cry out once when something pricked her. She sank back into silence until they emerged at his cabin, tucked in a cluster of pines.

He stopped one more time and listened for a full minute before he was satisfied. Jane was already sliding to the ground, landing with a hard jolt. She tipped her head up to look at him, still on the horse, and he was struck by how small she was, backed by the sprawl of forest behind her. The monster's wife had seemed bigger in his memory, stony faced at the trial, insistent that she knew nothing, stalwart in her lies.

"Go inside," he said.

"Where…? What will you do?"

"See to the horse."

She hesitated only for a moment and then walked to the wood-sided cabin, letting herself in through the unlocked front door. He climbed off Rosie and set about removing her saddle and letting her into the fenced area where Bud, the placid gelding, greeted her from the three-sided shelter. Though every muscle in him screamed its displeasure, he took the time to dump some feed into Rosie's bucket and quickly wipe her down and tend to the scratch on her flank.

"Thanks, girl," he said. "You got us out of a real mess."

As he limped to the cabin, he saw Jane watching him through the window, standing back a bit as if she was afraid. Of him? Or the creature she'd been married to?

And what exactly was he supposed to do with her? Everything in him wanted to toss her out into the woods and let her work out her own reconciliation with Wade. She'd made her choices; she should live with them.

But the other part of him, the small part that was still clinging to some sort of goodness and decency, would not allow that. During one of her infrequent moments of sobriety, their mother, Phoebe, would kiss her three children—his older sister, Claire, Mitch and Wade— and tell them, "You all got more than enough goodness in you." He was not sure now, when everything inside him felt dead and desiccated. He forced his legs to carry him away from his horses. He would let her stay until he figured something out, knowing it would have made his mother smile. Besides, he thought, as he crossed the porch, if Wade really was coming for Jane, she would be the perfect bait.

And he would need every advantage he could get to catch his brother again, one final time.

Jane stood in the tiny front room of Mitch's cabin, examining the cramped, moonlit space. The living area consisted of a hand-carved wooden rocking chair next to a standing lamp that did not work when she flipped on the wall switch. A shadowed alcove looked to be a minuscule kitchen across from an open door through which she glimpsed a neatly made bed and an attached bathroom. She was surprised he allowed himself the luxury of running water, this hermit of a man.

But she could understand his craving for solitude. When the threats started coming during the trial—the rocks through the window, animal blood spattered across her front porch—she too had desperately wanted to disappear among the trees, somewhere, anywhere to escape the hatred. It seemed to Jane that she'd lost everyone—

her mother, who'd been forced to quit her job as an elementary school aide before her lethal stroke, her sister, who cut off contact for the sake of her own family, and her friends—until there was nothing left for Jane but the tiny God-breathed life growing inside her. She'd promised herself that Ben would live and thrive far away from Wade and his terrible legacy.

"He won't ever be a part of your life," she'd whispered over his downy head, soothing him in the one luxury she allowed herself in her run-down rented room, a secondhand glider rocker. Of all the possessions she'd abandoned, she missed that beat-up old rocker the most, patched arm, stained cushion and all.

The twin pangs of despair and panic bit at her, through the numbing chill that stiffened her limbs. It was too late for Jane, but her son would have his chance at a normal life. *Lord, please help me save Ben. Please.*

Arms wrapped tight around herself, she continued her perusal. There was nothing on the walls, no prints or paintings, no family photos, only blank wood panels. In the corner was a long shelf that ran the length of the wall, about five feet, crowded with something she could not make out in the gloom. She would have moved closer, but her legs were trembling so badly she stayed put until Mitch entered.

He pulled the heavy curtains closed and shut and locked the door and did the same with the rear exit in the kitchen. Then he turned on a lantern and activated a generator, which hummed to life.

"We'll stick to lantern light, except in the bathroom. Water will be hot in a bit. Go shower. I'll toss a clean towel in the door."

The veritable avalanche of words from this taciturn man unsettled her. "But…but you need medical attention."

"I don't."

She'd leave that issue for now. "We have to call the police."

"No phone."

She gaped. "You don't have a landline, either?"

No cell service. No landline. No communication. It had been a long time before she'd realized the place Wade had purchased for their idyllic, romantic homestead had no cell coverage. And she had never so much as suspected he'd chosen it for that very reason until the end. Not idyllic—isolated. Not romantic—remote. She swallowed the bile that rose in her throat.

He jutted his chin at her. "Gonna get the heater started. It will warm quickly." He cleared his throat. "I'll, uh, find you something to wear while you shower."

"Let me bandage your head at least."

"Don't want your help." He said it without looking at her.

I don't want yours, either, she longed to say. No, she did not want it, but she and Ben needed Mitch Whitehorse desperately.

Wade had gone on the run for a short while after his crimes were brought to light, and it had only been through the sheer grit and determination of his older brother that he'd been arrested and brought back for trial. Now Wade had returned to kill Mitch and make good on his promise that Jane would be his wife forever, his property—his or no one's. The thought of being owned by Wade Whitehorse made her nauseous. The shivering now controlled her as her deepest fear began to grow roots down into her soul.

What would happen if Wade discovered she'd had his son? She'd been careful, excruciatingly meticulous about keeping Ben away from the public eye, but if Wade found out… Panic made her dizzy, and she clutched the back of the rocking chair.

Mitch loomed closer, dark eyes like pools of ink in the lamplight. He was so tall, features sharp and chiseled, his hair tar black. The glow caught in the rippled skin of his cheek, the scar caused, she knew, when Wade struck his brother full on in the face with a length of metal chain. It was a blow that probably would have ended the life of a weaker man. "Should you…sit down?" he said. The tone was not especially tender as it was neutral. For a man who believed the worst about her, it was the best she could hope for.

"I'm all right. I'll take that shower." She could not resist tossing over her shoulder, "Don't collapse while I'm in there, all right?"

She heard his annoyed grunt and hid a smile. It was going to be the greatest challenge of her life to convince Mitch that she was not the person he thought her to be. Judging from his granitelike stubbornness, it might just be an impossible task.

God had promised that nothing could separate her and Ben from His love, even those terrible crimes of her husband's. It was the promise she'd clung to when there was nothing but hatred everywhere she looked. God loved them both unequivocally, she knew with every breath she took. He'd entrusted Ben to her to keep her son safe and as far away from Wade as possible.

Mommy's going to come for you soon, Ben bear, and it's going to be all right.

If only she could make herself believe it.

FIVE

Mitch held the clothes up to the lantern light. There was no way Jane would be able to wear anything of his. The best he could do was scrounge up his smallest sweatshirt, which would no doubt hang down past her knees. And socks. Those would go up over her shins, so he figured she'd be covered and dry. It was the best he could do.

He found a clean towel. Quick as he could, he cracked the bathroom door and shoved the pile inside, yanking it closed before he changed into dry jeans and a long-sleeved flannel shirt. Every movement cost him a ripple of pain through his back. The side of his head felt like someone was striking it with a steel mallet, but at least he was dry. The space heater purred, and his own shivering had slowed. Using his mother's dented old kettle, he set the water on to boil. The shower was still running. Easing on a black slicker and a baseball cap, he grabbed his rifle and slipped out into the night.

The best practice would be to climb to the top of the rock ridge, which would give him a view of the hills below, but he was not sure he was steady enough to accomplish it, and the view would be clouded by the falling rain. He settled for doing a long, slow circle and checking for any signs that his brother had somehow persevered through the mud. There were no such indications, and the best tell of all was that Rosie and Bud were quiet and placid. Calmed somewhat, he hobbled back to the cabin.

Jane screamed when he entered.

He held up his palm, the rifle slung over his shoulder. "Just me. Property's secure."

She clutched the sweatshirt in a terrified fist, the fabric dwarfing her small frame. It took a few seconds for her voice to start working again. "Sorry. I thought…"

He knew what she'd thought, and he felt a stab of regret that he'd scared her. *No regret necessary*, he reminded himself sternly. *Remember who you're dealing with here.* The kettle finally began to boil, and he plopped bulky tea bags into two squat mugs and added the water. While it steeped, he ran over various plans about what to do with the woman who was wandering his house, swaddled in his clothes, twisting her long hair into a wet coil. When the tea was ready, he still had only a sketchy plan of attack.

Grabbing a bottle from the cupboard, he downed a couple of aspirin, swallowing them dry. He tossed the tea bags and carried the mugs, handing one to her.

She sniffed the steam. "What kind of tea?"

"Yarrow. My dad makes it."

She smiled. "He was kind, the one time I spoke to him on the phone. Does he live nearby?"

"Lives on a boat. He's paid as a ranch carpenter, but he's got a garden plot on the property."

Jane's smile vanished. "We have to tell him that Wade's escaped."

"I'll call him as soon as I can."

"What are we going to do?"

"Get you to the nearest US marshal."

Her breath hitched. "They won't be able to protect me."

"It's their job."

"They couldn't find him. Only you could. And they couldn't keep him in prison. He escaped from them."

"It's the only option."

She shook her head. "Do you figure Wade will leave you alone then? After you hand me over?"

"No. He's gonna come for me, and I'll send him back to prison or one of us will die. That's how it's gonna end, but you and the kid are not going to be in the middle of it."

Her chin went up. "Ben. His name is Ben."

Ben. Wade's son. *How much of his father did he inherit?* Mitch wondered. *Don't go there, Mitch. You share genes with your brother, too.* "Where is he?"

She remained stubbornly silent.

He let the quiet spool out for a few minutes, waiting for her to speak. Cop trick. She didn't. "Wade said you'd been storing things for him."

"What things?"

"My granddad's gun, for one."

She shook her head. "I didn't."

"Then how did he get the gun?"

"I have no idea."

He drank some tea. "Before daybreak, we'll go to the ranch and call the marshals."

Her throat worked convulsively, and then she took a deep breath. "Wade will find me, Mitch, no matter what kind of safe house they put me in. He'll find me, and he'll take Ben."

Her last words broke, and it made his gut go tight. He hardened himself against the feeling. *Remember what she is, whose she is.*

"Should have thought of that before you married the guy, right?" It was cruel, but what she'd let Wade do, turned a blind eye to, made her complicit. Just because her plans had backfired for some reason didn't mean he was going to let himself be manipulated.

The lamplight picked up the glittering sparks of moisture in her hair as she stared at him, small in her oversize clothes, but the ferocity in her eyes was bigger than life. "Go ahead and think that I'm stupid, gullible and blind. Believe me, I've thought all of those things and more. How did I not see Wade for what he was? I've wrestled with that every day of my life since the police showed up on my doorstep."

He shifted, not wanting to hear anything more, but she went on.

"Maybe I had a desperate need to be loved, or maybe it was low self-esteem or just plain insanity, but in the beginning I believed Wade was a good man, and I thought he loved me." She tipped her chin up to look at him. "Wasn't there a time when you believed your brother? When he fooled you?"

Fooled you. More times than Mitch could remember in their younger years. Wade was a master manipulator, and he'd bamboozled his own kin, misled their parents for decades, skated away from consequences by deceiving, charming, lying to teachers, cops and, yes, to Mitch also. Finally, he allowed one curt nod.

She sighed, shoulders slumping. "I would give anything to do it over again, to ask questions about where Wade went all those times he told me he was away on business trips. If I'd walked those acres he'd insisted were infested with rattlesnakes, I might have heard those women call for help. Instead I was asleep in my cozy little house, in my make-believe world." Her voice squeezed off, the barest glimmer of tears pooling, fingers clenched into white fists. "How do you think it feels to know I could have saved those women and didn't?"

The tears began to trickle down her face, paralyzing him, confusing him. Jane was his enemy just like Wade.

But the anguish she spoke of was one he'd experienced, too.

When he'd left for the police academy, he had intentionally walled his brother out of his life, leaving him loose to destroy, as Mitch knew deep down he would. He'd left it to other jurisdictions, other cops, until the damage was done, until lives had been lost.

How do you think it feels to know I could have saved those women and didn't? It was the same accusation he'd leveled at himself, too.

He could not order the mess of confusion in his thoughts, so he set down his mug and took the other from her trembling hand, putting them on the crate that served as a coffee table. "Lie down on the bed and get some sleep. I'll keep watch. We'll leave at oh four hundred. That's…"

"Four a.m. I know." She followed him to the bedroom. He took the old quilt down from the closet and laid it on the bed.

"It's cold back here. I'll move the heater in."

"Thank you," she said in a very small voice. She stood there for a moment, scanning the tiny room. "I'm sorry for the pain I know I've caused you by running here. Wade hurt you, too, probably more than me." Her chin went up then. "But I'm not sorry I came. I would do anything to save my son. He's all that matters, and, God willing, I'm going to protect Ben."

There it was again in her voice, the twined strands of

pain and strength, hints of anguish, an echo of a strange kind of certainty she had no right to. If she was telling the truth...

He brushed the thought away. He had no energy left to consider anything but the most pressing matters—keeping them both alive and getting her delivered safely to the US marshals. Then he would be free to go to war with his brother until they'd decided the winner once and for all.

She approached Mitch cautiously, shortly after midnight. He was sitting in the dark living room, the rocking chair pulled near the window, the rifle lying over his knees, so still she was not sure whether he was awake or asleep. The temperature had dropped, and she clutched the blanket around herself.

"Jane?" he said, making her jump.

"I came to take my turn at watch."

"No need. Go back to sleep."

"There is a need. You can't stay up all night. I'll watch for a couple of hours. I'll wake you if I see anything."

"No, you..."

"What? You think I can't use my two eyes as well as you use yours? Believe me, I've been looking over my shoulder for two years now. I'm pretty good at it."

He didn't answer.

She heaved out a breath. "Oh, right. You still think I'm somehow in league with Wade."

The room was dead quiet, save for the moan of the wind that skimmed the roof.

"Mitch, I risked my life to drag you into that boat. I could much more easily have let him kill you or never shown up here at all. No offense, but this isn't exactly the Ritz-Carlton." Her attempt at humor fell flat. He sat there, cradling the rifle like some monolithic statue. A sigh escaped her, and she turned to go.

"One hour," he said.

"What?"

"I'll sleep for one hour. Then wake me, if I'm not out here."

"Okay," she said. She ran a finger over the rocking chair. "I had an old banged-up glider rocker. Sitting there with Ben, even when he was crying..." She shrugged. "Those were the best moments of my life. I miss that rocker."

He hesitated a moment, as if he were about to speak, then took the rifle and checked out the window for one last look. She wandered the small space, over to the corner she had not examined earlier. Peering closer, she hardly managed to hold back an exclamation. The long rectangular board housed a train track, which wound through little snowcapped mountains. A miniature train stood ready, as if to start off on a journey, past the cluster of horses and the painstakingly painted trees.

Mitch stopped on his way to the bedroom.

"You like model trains?" she said.

He nodded. "Since I was a kid."

"Does it run?"

"Of course." There was a slightly offended tone in his reply. He reached past her and switched on the train. It slowly chugged to life and began its journey around the tracks. He watched it for a few minutes. From the corner of her eye, she caught an expression on his face that she could not decipher... Satisfaction, regret?

The longing for her son sprang to life so suddenly

it almost choked her. *Mommy, twain?* she could hear him say, pointing with his chubby finger when she'd risked taking him to the train station. He had not yet mastered the *r* sound, but his passion for trains was already well developed, and when she had extra money to spare there was no better way to please him than with the purchase of a new toy train to add to his meager collection. If there was no money, as there usually wasn't, they would watch the tracks, free entertainment. "Ben loves trains, too," she managed to say without crying.

They both watched the locomotive chug around until Mitch switched it off. "Wake me if there's anything and…"

"I know. One hour. Got it." She waited until he was almost through the door before she added, "And I promise I won't touch your train."

Again there was no answer from Mitch as he closed the door. She heard the bed springs groan as he eased his huge frame onto the mattress. As she was about to turn toward the rocking chair, she noticed the name painted in delicate gold letters on the engine… Paige Lynn.

She had only ever seen Mitch Whitehorse in the courtroom, austere and silent in his marshal's uniform, his glittering stare hard as diamond. Unmarried and childless as far as she knew. So who was Paige Lynn? And who, really, was Mitch Whitehorse, the immovable mountain with a soft spot for toy trains?

Doesn't matter who he is deep down, she told herself. She had to persuade him to help her, to make an ally out of an enemy.

Gathering the blanket around her, she eased into the rocking chair, listening to the wind, straining to hear any whisper of danger.

SIX

Mitch slept. He dreamed, as he often did, of a black snake rising from the water, fangs dripping. As the fleshy maw gaped toward him, he stood paralyzed, unable even to scream. He jerked to consciousness with a shout, grabbing out at the viper, only to find himself clutching Jane's wrist.

He let go and bolted from the bed so fast sparks danced in his vision. "I'm sorry," he mumbled.

"It's okay. You were muttering to yourself."

Great. And she heard.

"I have nightmares, too. I saw a counselor when I could, and she said it's the mind's way of processing what the heart can't."

He didn't answer, wiping the sweat from his forehead with his sleeve.

"Ben has them, sometimes. Night terrors, they're called."

Well, whaddya do about them? he wanted to ask but did not. As if she read his thoughts, she answered anyway.

"My mom used to sing me the 'Jesus Loves Me' song. Know it?"

He nodded.

"That's what I sing to myself and Ben when we have nightmares.

He shook his head with a grunt. "Figures."

"What?"

"That 'Jesus loves you' stuff. How can you believe that after what you've experienced?"

"I didn't for a long time. After Wade, I can't trust my own heart or head to separate what's truth from what isn't. God is the one thing, the only thing, I know is true." Her voice dropped to the barest whisper. "It's the only thing that keeps me alive."

He didn't know what to say to that. He'd heard it, of course, particularly from Aunt Ginny, Uncle Gus's wife, and from Pops, too, but did he believe it? No way. Some mythical, fanciful love from an invisible god was far away from the reality of his world—a mother who drank herself into the grave, and a brother who killed a series of women who had probably prayed with their very last breaths to a god who hadn't saved them.

He pulled on his boots and jacket before he noticed the time on his mother's old mantel clock. "It's three thirty," he snapped.

"Yes. I tried to wake you before, but you were sleeping soundly."

He grimaced. "You should have tried harder."

"I've heard it's a bad idea to disturb a hibernating bear."

Her face was serious, but there was a glint of humor in her eye.

Humor, incredible. It banked his ire. He sighed. "Yeah, well, I guess that's fair. Best get going soon. We'll take the horses."

"How long a ride is it to the ranch?"

"An hour, give or take. The trail winds along the coast. There are...exposed parts."

The fear flashed anew in her eyes, so he tried to disarm it. "We'll be okay. Hungry?"

"Yes. I didn't eat yesterday. You?"

"Yeah, but I'm not much of a cook. Got some cereal. Maybe some bread and canned things."

"May I try to fix us something?"

That threw him off. No one had cooked a meal just for him since Paige Lynn. The thought lashed through him. Her departure had cut a scar worse than the one on his face. "Uh, you don't need to do that."

But she had already taken his silence as assent and gone off to clatter around the kitchen. He used the time to feed and saddle the horses. Jane hadn't seemed like much of a rider, but Bud was placid and easy, as long as Rosie was there to take the lead. The air was rain washed and cold, which only aggravated his stiff muscles.

When he returned to the cabin, he was greeted by a tantalizing smell, which made his mouth water. He sat at the table, and Jane slid a plate of pancakes toward him and another for herself.

"There was no syrup, so strawberry jelly will have to do. You have a lot. Who made it?"

"I did."

She laughed.

"What's funny?"

"I'd never peg you for the jelly-making type."

He shrugged. "My mom showed me how." In one of the precious weeks when she wasn't intoxicated. The moment with her in the kitchen, up to his wrists in berries, was one of his dearest memories, but there was no point in sharing that. "Lots of wild berries up here in the summer. Strawberries and blackberries."

"Then I guess you do know a little something about food preparation."

"Only jelly, that's it. Dunno how to cook anything else."

She held out her hand to him.

He gaped, unsure.

"Okay if I pray?"

Was it? He didn't know.

He tried for a joke. "You should pray for a fancier meal, better digs."

She cocked her head. "I take things moment by moment. Right now I'm safe, my son is safe and I have a delicious pancake to eat with strawberry jelly. That's a whole lot to give thanks for."

Hesitantly, he took her small hand. It was cool, and the bones felt delicate, like a bird's. She said grace, ending with a soft amen.

He wanted to stare at her, to see if she was for real, this woman he'd been so certain about only a day earlier. She was pretending, assuming a facade, had to be, but he saw only earnest pleasure in her expression as she daintily ate the sticky pancake with a knife and fork.

He stacked one on top of the other and rolled, eating it sandwich style, which made her laugh again. "Ben does that, too."

"It's faster, eating them that way. We're always turning out early at the ranch."

"I used to sleep late, until…" She shrugged. "Anyway, I get up early now, too, and stay up late. Good thing Ben is a napper."

Ben, always, in her comments, in her thoughts—unless she was making the whole thing up to pull on his heartstrings. He helped her clean up and grabbed his rifle. "Ready?"

She swallowed and raised her chin. "I think so, but I'm not good on a horse."

"Bud's gentle. You just have to stay in the saddle."

"Story of my life," she said.

He had to smile at that. "You and me both," he said.

Jane clutched the saddle horn with one hand and the reins in another. Bud seemed content to amble along in the dark, staying close behind Rosie. Mitch kept their pace slow, stopping every so often to listen. Whenever he did, her skin crawled, picturing Wade tracking them, waiting for his chance. All she could hear was the crash of the water against the rocks, though fog obscured the ocean from view.

They'd been traveling a scant twenty minutes by her reckoning, along a road with sea cliffs on one side and grassland on the other. She'd put her own clothes back on, and they were still slightly damp, the clamminess chilling her deep down. A spray from the dew-spattered branches caught her in the cheek and trickled down her neck, freezing her skin inch by inch.

Mitch did not seem perturbed by the cold or the early hour, but she knew he had to be sore from their encounter with Wade. She was wrestling through whether or not she should ask him about his head when a shot echoed through the air. Jane would have screamed if she hadn't been trying so hard to remain on the horse. Mitch urged Rosie forward, Bud lurching behind. She'd barely kept her seat on the animal, fear pinching hard at her stomach.

"Get along, Rosie," he whispered urgently, guiding the horses forward behind an outcropping of rock. He stopped suddenly, sliding off Rosie and whirling toward her. Her heart slammed into her ribs as she took his hand and leaped from the horse. Mitch grabbed up both sets of reins.

"Come on."

She followed him as quickly as she could, stumbling over the rocks she could not see in the dark. He led the way deep into a fringe of shrubbery, which yanked at her hair. Pulling the reins, he guided the horses away from the trail and let them loose and pulled her to her knees next to him.

"Where did the shot come from?" she whispered.

"Behind us a ways, from the direction of my cabin."

"Shouldn't we be running for it?" She breathed through the shuddering fear.

"Trail is exposed over the ridge. He'd have an easy time picking us off." Mitch gripped her shoulder. "Quiet. Someone's coming."

She fought to breathe as she finally heard it for herself, the faint sound of hooves scuffling along the muddy trail. Wade, she knew, was an expert rider. He'd taken numerous lessons, and in fact, he'd met his first victim at the stables, a woman he'd imprisoned and killed after coercing her into handing over a large sum of money. It would be easy for him to ride the bumpy trail from the cabin to their hiding place with impressive speed.

Prickles danced over her skin, and she fought down the yelp of panic that threatened.

If she didn't make it out alive, what would happen to Ben? She could not rely on her sister to raise him, not with Wade an ever-present threat to her and her own children. Roxanne had moved to the East Coast, changed her name, phone numbers, email, everything.

Nana Jo, the precious woman who had agreed to come to Roughwater with her to tend to Ben while she chased down Mitch, would not be able to evade Wade, either. They were safe for now, in a trailer Jane had rented for them, since she was keeping her distance and Nana Jo was on the lookout for any sign of Wade. The tough-as-nails woman knew Jane's whole story and refused to be intimidated out of helping, but she was no match for Wade, especially after he'd found Nana's house, where Jane rented a room. Who? How? The questions threatened to overwhelm her until she forced the thought through the panic. *God loves Ben even more than I do. He will make a way for him, even if I'm not there.*

Forcing herself to stay quiet, she counted the seconds, listening to the rider coming closer. Mitch crawled on his belly to a patch between the rocks that was raised enough that he could aim his rifle toward the trail where the rider would soon emerge around the sharp bend.

He looked at Jane and forced the reins into her shaking palm. "Take Rosie and run."

Run where? The rocks closed in from every side, and she could barely make out the trail in the dark. Wade would find her in moments.

"Go," he said fiercely. "Walk her away from the path before you mount. She'll find a way down to the beach. Head north. You'll find an inlet with a dock and a couple of boats. One is my dad's. Go now, as far away as you can."

Fear squeezed her insides. On shaking legs, she sidled up to Rosie and tugged at the reins. The horse shook her neck and snorted, seemingly reluctant to leave Mitch and Bud.

"Come on, Rosie," she whispered.

Rosie danced from hoof to hoof.

The crunch of rock underfoot grew louder, closer, then slowed.

For a fleeting moment, she hoped Wade would turn around, give up on his pursuit.

Mitch aimed his rifle, squinting slightly with one eye.

There was a soft squeak of a saddle as the rider slid off his horse, coming toward them, one slow step at a time.

SEVEN

Mitch wedged his cheek to the stock, pressed with steady, even pressure taking the slack out of the trigger, ready for the shot as soon as he could be sure. Something didn't feel right. Wade was insane, but he was not stupid. He knew Mitch was expecting an attack. Further, he knew the earlier gunshot had given him away. So why march straight forward into the line of fire?

Blood pounded in his temples, and his eyes burned as he stared at the point where Wade would emerge into view. Behind him he heard Jane struggling to get Rosie to obey, but he dared not turn his head to help her.

One more step, then the figure obscured by darkness stepped into view. Mitch increased the pressure on the trigger until he heard a familiar whistle.

"If you're gonna shoot, don't get the shirt. It's new," came the whispered drawl as Liam Pike walked slowly into view.

He breathed out a whoosh of relief and lowered the rifle. He felt Jane edge beside him.

"It's okay." He took the reins from her and led them back onto the path. "This is Liam Pike. He works at Roughwater Ranch."

Liam wore his customary grin, the tousled red curls and stubbled chin as roguish as ever, but Mitch immediately detected the underlying gravity in his friend's tone, the tightness of his shoulders. Liam was his brother, though not genetically, Liam's only sister, Helen, close as his own. So too was Chad Jaggert, another member of the ranch family, Uncle Gus and Aunt Ginny's unofficially adopted brood. Keeping their noise to a minimum, he led them all back into the screen of foliage.

"Heard a shot," Mitch said.

Liam nodded. "I rode up to your cabin to check on you when we got a call from the marshal that Wade escaped. He was hiding behind your woodpile. He took a shot, but he's not a proper marksman." Liam huffed out a breath. "He shouldn't have been able to get the drop on me."

Mitch caught the emotion behind the easygoing Southern-boy facade. In the past, Liam Pike, former Green Beret, would never have missed the sounds of an ambush, but that was before a disease eroded his hearing, leaving him deaf in one ear and with damage in the other. He could hide his shame and frustration from everyone except for Mitch. Mitch offered a casual shrug. "Missed, that's all that matters."

"My reflexes are still good," Liam said, his cocky grin back in place. "Lithe as a cat." His gaze shifted to Jane, and he angled a questioning eyebrow.

"Jane Reyes," Mitch said. He left the rest unsaid. Liam's calculating glance told Mitch he'd put it all together. This was the former wife of a sadistic killer. "She says Wade is after her."

He felt her stiffen beside him. "He is," she said. "He almost killed both of us on the beach last night."

Liam tapped his own temple and looked at Mitch's battered forehead. "Souvenir?"

Mitch nodded. "To go with the scar on my cheek. I'm taking her to the ranch until the marshal arrives."

"He rolled onto the ranch an hour ago." Liam wiggled his cell phone at Mitch. "You'd know that if you had this clever device we like to call a satellite phone."

Jane shot him a "that's what I told him" smile. He ignored it. "Did the marshal come with you?"

Liam looked away for a moment. "I didn't tell him where I was going. He was making calls when I left."

Mitch wondered why Liam had decided to leave the marshal behind, but the question could wait until later. "Pops?"

"I called your father and told him. He's okay, taking precautions."

Mitch felt his muscles relax a fraction. "Figure Wade's still around?"

He shrugged. "Fifty-fifty. Gonna be dawn soon, and I tracked him headed away from here. My guess is he's gonna cut the horse loose and head to a car. Then again, he really hates you, so he might not be making prudent choices."

"I'll check the local stables to see if he rented a horse. Could have stolen it. Which marshal is assigned to this?"

"Guy by the name of Foley," Liam answered.

Mitch exhaled, biting back a comment.

"Know him?"

"Yeah."

"You're not best buddies?"

Mitch didn't reply. Liam shot another quick glance at Jane and then away. He'd save his questions for later. No way was a Green Beret going to share information in front of a potential hostile. Was that what Jane was? He didn't know for sure, but he wished anybody but Al Foley was heading up the operation. They had a history, and it wasn't one he wanted to revisit. Ever.

One problem at a time, he told himself.

He helped Jane astride Bud and swung into the saddle on Rosie. "We'll get there as quick as possible. Most likely Wade has left, like Liam said."

"Is Liam coming, too?" Jane turned in the saddle to look for him and gasped. "He's already gone."

Of course he was. Separately they had a much better chance of evading Wade and even tracking him. Liam's hearing might not be acute, but he had plenty of remaining skill. A formidable fighter, a worthy brother.

Mitch had a feeling he was going to be calling upon all of Liam's skills very soon indeed.

Jane endured the ride, which took nearly two hours since they stopped frequently to listen for sounds of pursuit. The sense of being stalked and her rudimentary riding skills left her muscles screaming. Finally, as dawn broke, they emerged from the woods at the edge of a vast plateau that overlooked the misty Pacific Ocean. The sun lightened the sky from slate to silver, outlining a sprawling set of Mission-style buildings. At the entrance to the grounds was a sign spelling out Roughwater Ranch in iron letters. The stucco walls of the main house were topped with bronzed tiles on the roof, the central structure towering over the lower parts, backed by wooded green hills to the rear. It was gorgeous and not at all the type of place where she would have pictured a roughened cowboy like Mitch Whitehorse.

An unmarked car was parked in the driveway. Jane had spent enough time during Wade's trial being followed by police that she recognized a cop car when she saw one. They'd protected her from the press and the public hatred until the moment Wade was convicted, and then she'd had to face the aftermath alone. Even when her mother had the stroke that would later end her life, Jane had to disguise herself and sneak into the hospital to avoid reporters eager to flay her in the public eye. With the exception of her precious friend Nana Jo, she'd been completely alone ever since.

And now the horror was starting up all over again. Jane's breath caught. Mitch would deliver her and Ben to the marshal. Then it would be a life spent in safe houses and watching over her shoulder until the moment Wade found her again, as she knew he would. Trying to keep her legs from collapsing, she slid off Bud before Mitch could dismount from Rosie. If he figured he would hand her over like a Christmas goose, he was in for a surprise. God had given her Ben, and she would do right by him until there was no breath left in her body. Surreptitiously she tried to smooth her rumpled jacket and wipe a smudge from the leg of her damp jeans.

Liam approached along a wide graveled road that bordered a split-rail fence. He led an elegant black horse by the reins. Somehow he'd managed to beat them back to the property unnoticed. He politely took the reins from her and Mitch.

"I'll see to the horses. Join you in a few." He left them to make their way into the main house. She forced her stiff joints to keep up with Mitch's long-legged stride. He let himself in the ornate front door and held it for her to enter, chivalry she had not expected.

The place was all dark woods, white walls and burnished Spanish tile floors. Past a sturdy stand that displayed an oiled saddle, she followed Mitch through an arched entry into a massive dining area. The interior begged for her attention, particularly the display of orchids thriving along the windowsill, but she was drawn instead to the three men and one woman seated at a long, solid wood table. Two of the men stood when she entered; the one in uniform did not.

The small woman with the silver pixie cut, energetic and lithe, walked to Jane, solemnly extending a palm. "Hello. You must be Jane. I'm Mary Knightly, but everyone who sets foot on Roughwater Ranch winds up calling me Aunt Ginny." She did not exactly smile, but she quirked a look at Mitch. "Liam called earlier. You could have called, too, with the cell phone we gave you at Christmas. You remember that present, right?"

Mitch sighed. "Yes, ma'am. Liam already roasted me about that."

"It's still in the box, isn't it?" When Mitch didn't answer at first, she arched an eyebrow. "Well?"

"Yes, ma'am," he said, sounding like a chastised little boy.

Now Jane saw Ginny allow a slight smile. "Mitch will tell you his determined streak comes from the proud Cherokee ancestry on his father's side, but I think it's a condition called stubbornness that all the men inherit around here."

"And the women," the older man piped up. He too extended a calloused hand, his dark eyes genial but guarded. "I'm Gus Knightly, Uncle Gus to her Aunt Ginny. Mitch's mom was my big sis." He gestured to a young man whose sober expression left him unreadable.

"This is Chad Jaggert. You've met Mitch, our nephew, and Liam. Chad's our unofficial son, along with Liam."

Chad fingered the cowboy hat in his hands and nodded politely. "Ma'am."

The marshal got to his feet and cleared his throat as if interrupting.

"And this is Marshal Al Foley."

Foley nodded. He was a stocky man, muscled rather than fat, perhaps a few years older than Mitch and a head shorter. Fatigue lines bracketed his mouth, and the bags under his eyes were pronounced. "Ms. White-horse."

"Reyes," Jane corrected instantly.

"Ms. Reyes," he went on with a hint of something in his tone. "I'm sure we both appreciate the Knightly family for trying to make you feel at home, but this isn't a social occasion. Come sit down."

"I'd rather stand."

He glowered. "Stand, then. There's more at stake here than your comfort."

Mitch rolled a shoulder. "We've been riding for hours, and she's not used to that."

The marshal's mouth twitched. "Guess you being retired, you're not, either, huh, Whitehorse? Living the quiet life here in Driftwood away from the action?"

Mitch didn't reply, but Jane saw a vein jump in his jaw.

"You two used to work together?" Gus said.

"More alongside each other," Mitch said.

Foley's gaze stayed on him for a moment before traveling to Jane.

"I'm sorry if this is an inconvenient time, but I need to talk to you immediately."

"Not immediately," Ginny said.

The marshal and Mitch both jerked a questioning look at her.

"Her clothes are damp." Ginny took Jane by the forearm, guiding her away. "She needs to get something dry on. We'll be back in a minute."

"But…" the marshal sputtered.

Ginny paid him no mind and sailed along with Jane in tow. They reached a bedroom with two twin beds covered by neat hand-stitched quilts. "I'd give you some of my things, but as Gus says, I'm 'fun sized,' so mine won't fit. Helen leaves clothes here for when she visits unexpectedly." Ginny rummaged in the drawers and pulled out a pair of jeans and a T-shirt that read "Love me, love my horse."

"I…I appreciate it very much," Jane said. "But I'd better get back to the marshal. He's…"

Ginny leveled a look at Jane that dried up all her words. "Jane, I don't know what your story is, what you did or didn't know about Wade Whitehorse. I suppose that's not my business anyway, but I will never allow a man, any man, to boss a woman under my roof. Am I clear?" Her eyes sparked blue fire.

Jane closed her open mouth. "Yes, ma'am," she mumbled.

"Call me Aunt Ginny," she said with a mischievous grin. "Bathroom's through there. There's an ancient phone if you need it. Come out when you're settled. I'll find you something to eat."

She left, leaving the bedroom door open and Jane standing there, clutching the offered clothing. Hastening to the bathroom, Jane stripped away her sodden garments and pulled on the borrowed items. She and

Helen must be roughly the same dimensions, since the clothes fit well enough. She balled up the wet ones and put them in a corner of the bathroom, and then she all but ran to the phone, dialing Nana Jo's number on the clunky push-button pad. After four interminable rings, Nana Jo answered.

"Jane, I've been worried sick. Are you all right?" Nana Jo's voice was breathless and high.

"I'm okay. Wade found me, but I got away."

Silence followed by a weak sigh. "Oh, Jane. I can't believe this is starting all over again. Should I pack?"

"No," she said savagely. "I'm getting help."

"From Wade's brother? But doesn't he think…?"

"That I'm complicit, yes, but I am going to convince him to help me." *I have to.*

"Jane, maybe we should go. My cousin in Idaho…"

"Nana, I can't, don't you see? There's nowhere to run from this. I have to make a stand if Ben's ever going to have a life. If you can just watch him a little longer…" She hated the pleading that crept into her voice.

"You know I will as long as I can."

"It will be safe if Wade doesn't know about Ben. Can I talk to him for a minute?"

"Sure." In a moment Jane heard the sound of a child's breathing on the line. Her breathing hitched hard. "Hey, Ben Bear, it's Mommy."

"Hi, Mommy," he said.

Tears crowded her eyes, and she thought she might not be able to squeeze out anything further. "What are you doing with Nana Jo?" she managed.

"Twains."

"You're playing trains? That sounds like fun. I am going to see you real soon, okay? I miss you."

She heard Nana Jo prompting him to say goodbye.

"I love you, Ben Bear."

"Wuv you, Mommy."

Wuv you, Mommy. Tears slipped down her cheeks as she hung up the receiver. Turning to the door, she started to see Mitch, standing uncertainly, dark eyes watching. He held a fluffy pink towel that Aunt Ginny must have figured she might want.

Having him witness her uncloaked fear and pain made her suddenly angry.

"Are you surprised to see the monster's wife can cry?" she snapped.

His mouth opened as if he were about to say something. Instead he closed it, put the towel gently down on the closest bed and walked away.

EIGHT

I love you, Ben Bear.

It was the combination of the words and the anguish in the tone that made the scene stick in Mitch's mind as he returned to the dining room. *All right*, he told himself. *So she loves her kid. Maybe she changed after she gave birth.* Women did, he knew, and men. Becoming a parent altered people in intangible ways. He used to daydream about how he would be different when he and Paige Lynn were married, until he'd learned the hard way that for the Whitehorses, dreams evaporated quickly but hardships stuck around.

He should have learned that lesson early on. His own mother had given up alcohol while pregnant, according to Mitch's father, but the changes just wouldn't stick, not for Claire, Wade or Mitch, or her husband. Addiction gripped Phoebe with voracious fangs, and love and prayers and pleading could not free her.

Again he felt the coin flipping in his gut between Jane, the monster's ex-wife, and Jane, a woman willing to do anything to protect her baby boy. Which was the truth?

"Doesn't matter," he told himself. Whoever she was, Jane Reyes and Ben would be safer in the custody of the

US marshals. He returned to find Aunt Ginny sliding a plate of muffins onto the table. His stomach growled, but there was no way he was going to eat if Foley didn't. Chad had gone to sit in a shadowed corner of the living room next to one of the ranch dogs, which was about as social as he got with strangers. Liam had no such reservations about the company. He set about loading up a plate and slid into a seat next to Uncle Gus, making sure, Mitch knew, that his right ear was toward the marshal. Liam didn't want to miss a word of the whole situation.

Jane joined them, face now dry and composed. Aunt Ginny handed her the platter, and she accepted a muffin with a grateful nod.

"Blueberry muffins are the only kind of fancy thing I can make. Gus is the cook around here."

Gus winked. "Don't let her fool you. She can cook most anything if she studies up on it. We ate beef stew for a week solid while she practiced that recipe, and now it's restaurant quality."

She pinked and waved a dismissive hand at her husband. "I'm a decent cook, I guess, but I've decided to take up baking as a hobby. I've only recently started on muffins, so it's only been two days of eating those."

Liam laughed. "Nothing wrong with these muffins, Aunt Ginny." He helped himself to a mug of coffee to go with it.

Foley fidgeted. "Like I said, Miss Reyes, we need to talk. I got the details of Wade's attack on the beach from Mitch. The guy at the stables down the road says Wade politely returned the horse he rented an hour ago, got into a car, which he can't describe, and headed away from town, but he may be back, so we have to get you into protective custody as soon as possible."

"I appreciate that, Marshal Foley, but it isn't what I want."

He frowned. "It isn't what anyone wants, but it will keep you alive until we recapture your husband."

"My ex-husband," she corrected again. "And forgive me, but I'm not confident that you're going to catch him."

"We'll catch him," Foley said. "We did last time."

"You caught him because of Mitch."

Foley's eyes went flat as a mile of empty road. He stared directly at Jane without sparing a glance for Mitch. "He's not a marshal anymore."

"I know, but he's the only person who ever got close enough, the only person who can."

Foley snorted. "Because they're kin?"

Something in the way he said it made Mitch's blood boil. The hatred in Foley's eyes took him back to the days before the capture. Foley, the marshal tasked with capturing Wade, had sat fuming when Mitch was brought in by Foley's superiors since Foley hadn't been able to do the job. The hatred was worsened by other events that had only stoked Foley's fury at Mitch. "You know how I feel about Wade."

"Do I? Took you long enough to capture him in the first place, didn't it, once you were finally pressured into joining the manhunt?"

"And I hear it took you the space of one routine prison transfer to let him escape," Mitch snarled.

Now both men were on their feet. Gus and Liam stood, too, wary, watching. Chad stopped stroking the dog's belly, frozen and alert.

"Simmer down, both of you," Gus said. "This is a conversation, purely. The important thing is the safety of this young woman."

They all remained standing except Jane and Aunt Ginny.

"Please sit down," Aunt Ginny said. "I feel like I'm in the middle of a bad spaghetti Western. Sit, sit," she clucked.

They did, but Mitch had to force his muscles to obey. The ice-pick pain stabbing his temple did not help.

Jane said calmly, "Marshal Foley, I would like to hear the details of Wade's escape, if I may."

"No point in it," Foley said.

"Still, I want to know."

"I can call in a favor and ask someone else in the marshal's office," Mitch put in.

Foley stared him down. "The details are me and another marshal were transferring Wade Whitehorse in a van to another prison, since he kept getting roughed up in spite of the warden's efforts to keep him isolated. En route, we rolled across a spike strip. The van overturned, knocking my partner unconscious and trapping me in a jammed seat belt. Wade escaped. End of story."

End of the part he was willing to share.

"So Wade had help," Jane said.

Foley went still. "Yes." After a beat he added, "Let's just put it out there. We looked hard for you, Miss Reyes. Couldn't find you until you showed up in Driftwood."

"You were looking for me to warn me?" Jane said. Mitch saw the realization rise in the silver surface of her eyes. "No, not to warn me. You don't care about me that much. You thought I helped him escape, didn't you?"

Foley jutted his chin. "The marshals are tasked with recovering fugitives. It's our job. Doesn't matter what we think."

"I can tell by your tone, by your questions, exactly

what you think." Jane stood, one slender hand braced on the table. "Find Wade. I pray that you do before anyone else dies, but I won't go to a safe house."

"Ms...." Foley started, but she shook her head.

"And for the record, I'll state it one more time." Her face was haggard, exhausted, but not defeated, not entirely. "I am not an ally to Wade Whitehorse. As a matter of fact, I never was." She went down the hall. He heard the bathroom door shut and lock.

Jane braced herself against the marble vanity, avoiding looking in the mirror. She knew what she'd see there—fear, doubt, rage, a woman with few options and even fewer friends.

"Doesn't matter," she muttered, splashing water on her face. "I have my son," she said to her reflection. "That's all I need." Ben was a gift beyond her wildest imagining, proof positive that God was with her in spite of her massive failure. Clinging to the cool stone, she tried to put together a plan.

Mitch would not help her.

The marshal did not believe her, and she did not know if she could trust him.

Nana Jo could not stay with Ben in the tiny trailer she'd rented them outside town for much longer. She'd have to run. Again. To start over and make a whole new identity once more, only she could not ask Nana Jo to come with her this time. The woman had a cozy home, her own life to live, a church family, and no one deserved to take on the label of a fugitive.

Certainly not her sweet boy.

But what was the choice? Whom could she turn to? Mitch had been her last and only hope. Once again she realized how much Wade had taken from her, the terrible price she and Ben continued to pay every moment of every day.

A small tap sounded on the door. Forcing a composed look, she opened it.

Aunt Ginny was there. "Come into the kitchen. Have some coffee and muffins."

"I..." Jane started, stopping abruptly as her throat swelled shut with grief.

Aunt Ginny squeezed her hand. "You have decisions to make, but let's go one at a time. Right now, it's time for food. Then you'll have strength for the next best decision."

Jane blinked back tears, clutching the warm hand that squeezed hers. In a daze, she allowed herself to be led to the kitchen and guided onto a stool at the island, which faced a stove settled into a stone-covered alcove. The floors were the same dark hardwood, reflected by the pendant lights. Behind her was another massive wood table, large enough for the whole Roughwater clan, a clay pitcher holding a spray of mums adding to the homey feel.

An iPad was open on the countertop, a video paused on the screen.

"I'm in week two of my online baking class. We're done with muffins, and speaking of which, you didn't take a morsel of the one I served you earlier." She slid one on a plate to Jane, along with a mug of coffee. "Liam's really excited because next week is pies. Mitch and Gus, and Pops, Mitch's father, could care less. They'll eat whatever you put in front of them including the paper plates without noticing. Chad hardly eats at all. Do you like to cook?"

"I did," she said. "Once upon a time." Now she was happy just to make macaroni for Ben. A plate of mac and cheese and sliced apples shared with her son was a God-given feast.

"If you're around next week, you can help with pies."

Jane smiled and blew out a breath. "Thank you for your hospitality. It's brave of you to even allow me in the door."

"I know a little bit about betrayal, honey, especially the kind where you're the last to know. My first husband, well, let's just say he was an unfaithful man and a liar to boot, and I didn't have an inkling. Even his family realized exactly what was going on, and none of them said a word. It humiliates a person, doesn't it?"

Jane could only nod, grateful beyond belief that this woman understood, at least in some small way.

She sighed. "It was especially painful since I wanted children more than anything, only I couldn't conceive, but Lex went on to father three kids with his other women. It just never seemed right to me, nor fair. It wasn't in the plans for Gus and me, either." She shook her head. "Not bragging, but I would have been a great mother."

Jane smiled. "Yes, Aunt Ginny. I am sure you would."

Aunt Ginny reached out a finger and gently touched the cross that hung around Jane's neck, her grandmother's sent to her by her sister, though there was no return address on the package, a gift that both sustained her and broke her heart at the same time. "You believe?"

Jane nodded. "It's the only thing I can do."

"The only thing that matters," Ginny said with a smile. "So that makes us sisters in Christ, you and me. I could use a sister with all these men around."

"I…I can't have a sister anymore. It's too dangerous for people to be in my life."

The morning sun bedazzled the kitchen, lighting a

shower of silver in Ginny's hair and traveling across the counter, bathing it in a buttery glow.

"It's risky, living life together, and horrible and awful and wonderful and perplexing. That's why we weren't meant to do it alone." She squeezed Jane around the shoulders and whispered in her ear. "That's what I keep telling that stubborn Mitch, anyway." She hopped off the bar stool and returned with the coffeepot to top off Jane's mug.

Uncle Gus came in with Liam, followed by Foley and Mitch.

"More muffins?" Liam asked hopefully.

Ginny offered up another on a napkin.

Mitch's dark brows were knitted together. Foley didn't look one bit happier.

Foley tucked a thumb into his utility belt. "Have you heard from Bette Whipple?"

The name shot right through Jane like an arrow, cleaving the tender membranes of her heart that she'd thought were healed. Bette Whipple, Wade's only surviving victim, the one who had been freed by the police before Wade could return to kill her, too. "No," she whispered. "Is she…okay? Did you tell her Wade has escaped?"

"We tried, but she's fallen off the radar. I wondered if somehow you two had connected over the years."

"No," Jane said. "I wrote her a letter, just one."

"Telling her what?"

Jane swallowed hard. "Apologizing that I didn't know, for the things I should have noticed." *For the pain I might have saved her.* "You have to notify her."

"We have people working on that. My job is to get you to a safe house."

"No," she said again.

"You gonna stick with that? You're making the wrong choice."

"But I have the right to make it."

Mitch cocked his head, silent and considering. She did not know what he thought, could not concern herself with it. He would not help her—that was all she needed to know.

"Where will you go?" Foley demanded. "Can I at least be in on that?"

She shrugged. "I don't know."

"She'll stay here today, anyway," Aunt Ginny said.

Jane shook her head. Oh, how she wished she could sink into the comfort that this home, this woman, offered, but she could not risk it, or them. "Thank you, but I—"

Ginny was undeterred. "You need a day to rest, eat. We'll wash your clothes, get you a new cell phone."

Foley's eyes rounded. "Anyone who helps this woman becomes a target." He turned to Mitch. "And in case you forgot, Wade showed up here in Driftwood to kill you, Mitch. You wanna risk the people around you getting caught in the cross fire?"

"We've got his back," Liam said, all the humor gone from his face.

Gus nodded. "Plenty of eyes and guns around here. Nothing is going to happen to my family."

"You're deluding yourselves. Wade Whitehorse is unlike any evil you've ever known."

"No," Mitch said quietly. "I know exactly who I'm dealing with."

And so do I, Jane thought with a quiver deep down in her belly. *That's why I have to get Ben and run.*

NINE

Mitch led Foley to the door.

"You're making a mistake," Foley said, "and you know it."

Mitch shook his head. "Like she said, it's her decision to make."

Foley snorted. "Typical."

He could say it, bring up Foley's past humiliation, the day his frustration had led him into a bar and he'd drunk himself to stumbling. Mitch had happened upon him, heading for his car. No way he was going to let the man drive drunk, but arresting him would ruin his career, so Mitch had hauled him back to his place, dumped him on the sofa and let him sleep it off. Next morning Foley was gone, but the shame Foley must have felt at being rescued by Mitch was clearly not. Mitch kept his peace as they squared off for a moment. "Say it, Foley," Mitch said at length. "Might as well get it off your chest." Liam approached quietly behind, close enough to let Mitch know he had backup and far enough that he wasn't butting in.

"You were always content to sit back and let others stick their necks out. You didn't even get involved in little brother's life until he'd killed three people."

"You would have done things differently if Wade was your brother?"

"Yeah, I would have taken responsibility and tracked him, at least. You always knew he would get around to murder, and you did nothing to prevent it."

Mitch let the recrimination roll through him along the well-worn paths of his soul. Foley was right. Mitch should have kept tabs on his brother's activities, should have known the inevitable would happen, but instead he'd walled himself away behind his other duties, aloof, avoiding any mention of his brother, refusing a cell phone except for work purposes, moving as far from their hometown in Arizona as he could manage.

Foley had fought to keep him off the case when Wade vanished after the trial. Roles reversed, Mitch might have done the same thing. Mitch Whitehorse would always be known as Wade's brother, and he would wear the stain of that evil forever. Judged, condemned.

Just like Jane, his heart told him suddenly. He stayed quiet, waiting for the rest.

"Are you too slow-witted after your years of retirement not to see the obvious?" Foley continued.

"Which is?"

"Jane could be working with Wade, coming here as a ruse, all ready with a sob story, to set you up so Wade could kill you."

"That's a lot of personal risk on her part just to kill me. Why would she stick her neck out?"

"Because you and I both know that Wade is capable of convincing people to do anything he wants, show them it's in their best interest to help him."

"She's smart enough to know she needs to stay away from him."

"She wasn't smart enough to avoid marrying him."

"You've been married three times. Didn't exactly make the right choices yourself."

Foley glared. "So it's just coincidence that she shows up on the beach just as Wade takes his shot?"

"She came to find me. Bad timing, not coincidence."

Foley grimaced. "You were a cop, Mitch. Use your head."

It was his heart more than his head that told him Jane's fear was not faked, her desperation not manufactured for his benefit, her tears for Ben earnest. But his heart wasn't a thing he could trust anymore, was it? And hadn't he been manipulated by the best?

He flashed back to a time decades before, when he was in his twenties, saving up to go to the police academy by loading hay in the summer. It was backbreaking work, but he didn't mind, as long as he got to see Paige Lynn in the evenings after she finished her waitressing shift. Wade had met him at the house one scorching summer night, asking for gas money to head into town and look for a job. Mitch told him he had none to spare. Wade claimed he understood, thanked Mitch even. Later that evening Mitch saw Wade setting off on the ten-mile walk between their home and town, sweating and dusty. Sympathy had won out, and Mitch peeled off a couple of twenties from the stash destined for savings and handed them to his grateful brother.

Paige Lynn told him later Wade brought his then girlfriend into the diner to town that same night and treated them both to a steak dinner with all the trimmings. The girlfriend's dad owned a gas station in the next town over, and Wade got all the free gasoline he wanted. Once Wade learned that Paige Lynn had reported what she'd seen to Mitch, he'd set about terrorizing her in a way that could never be proved. Calls from pay phones, flat tires, a dead bird in her handbag and finally…a lock of her little sister's hair mailed to her house. When she could not stand it anymore, she left both Mitch and the town far behind.

Jane's frightened silver eyes swam in his memory. Wasn't it possible that Wade had married a woman even more capable of lying than he was? He realized Foley was waiting for a response. "She's here for today. I'll keep you posted if anything happens."

Foley looked as if he would say more.

"Truth is, I don't care if Wade gets to you or not. I'm here to recapture him. Jane's a means to an end, and I'll get my man this time, with your cooperation or without it."

This time. Was that what this was? Foley's wounded pride over not being able to arrest Wade on his own? The shame of his drunken encounter with Mitch? *Jane's a means to an end.* Would he use her, leak her location to catch Wade? Shame burned in Mitch when he considered he'd thought of using Jane for bait as well. But that was before he understood what kind of woman she was, before he'd seen her anguish about Ben.

"Like I said, she's here for today."

Foley's mouth twitched, and he turned away.

An insidious thought occurred to Mitch as the marshal strode to his car. Wade had escaped two federal marshals with the help of an outside source.

Or could it have been an inside one? What if Wade had shown Foley it was in his best interest to work together, to help him with his plans?

En route, we rolled across a spike strip. The van over-

turned, knocking my partner unconscious and trapping me in a jammed seat belt. Wade escaped. End of story.

Was it? Wade had money somewhere—they'd never found all the funds he'd stolen from the women he killed. He clearly had enough to rent a horse, a car. He'd been dressed in good clothes when he'd tried to kill Mitch on the beach. Money talked. Did it talk loudly enough to bribe a marshal into working for a psychopath? Was the whole manhunt a farce?

Foley slid on a pair of sunglasses and drove too fast out of the gate. Mitch stared after him for a while, trying to separate what might be the facts from the bubbling mess of feelings.

Liam moved closer. "You trust Foley?"

"Don't trust anyone who isn't connected to this ranch."

"Good way to stay alive," Liam said. "But lonely."

Lonely, maybe, but smart. Then again, he'd brought Jane Reyes here to Roughwater Ranch, the one place he'd found peace, his sanctuary, his lifeline. All of a sudden, his past was roaring back into the present. His head ached. "All this talk is useless."

"As a screen door on a submarine," Liam drawled.

Mitch smiled in spite of himself. "You can drop the good old boy shtick with me."

"Whatcha mean? I'm just a simpleminded cowboy, Mitch."

"With an IQ of 145, which is genius level."

"Aw, shucks, who told you that?"

"Your sister."

Liam grinned. "Well, her IQ's higher than mine, so I guess you'd better trust her. Suits me to be a simple cowboy."

He'd never fully understood what happened in Liam's

life with his father, but he'd gotten a sense that Liam had put on many different identities and he was still in search of the right one. He allowed strangers to underestimate him, even welcomed it, but Mitch knew him too well—the parts he would allow Mitch to know, anyway.

"This is going to get messy," Mitch said. "Wade is not going to leave until he gets what he wants."

"Which is you in a pine box?"

"For starters."

"And Jane?"

"Not sure, but I'm gonna need both the genius and the cowboy to get through this, I think," Mitch said quietly.

"I'll be your posse. You can count on that."

Unable to put his gratitude into words, he nodded. Liam and Chad were better than brothers.

They returned to the house, and he bolted the door, the metal sliding home with an ominous clang.

Jane was grateful to be allowed to spend the day alone in the guest room Aunt Ginny had shown her earlier. She showered, wrapped up again in the borrowed clothes. A stab of panic shot through her as she realized she'd left her small pouch with her ID and ATM card in the bathroom in Mitch's cabin. She forced a calming breath. "I'll just have to retrieve it before I leave," she told herself. She'd found a canvas bag in the room with necessities—a hairbrush, toothbrush, tissues, as well as some plastic-wrapped muffins. She smiled.

After another shower, her body sagged with fatigue and she allowed herself to lie down on the bed. It was only midmorning, but it seemed like a lifetime since she'd survived being shot on the beach.

I'll never let you go.

Now that he knew Jane had made contact with Mitch, Wade had both his targets in one place. Tension knotted her stomach muscles.

She needed to plan, to figure out how to retrieve her pouch, pick up Ben and get out of Driftwood without being spotted by Wade or the marshal. She'd seen the expression on Mitch's face when Foley recounted the escape details, and she read the suspicion there, the same kind that roused her own instincts. Someone had helped Wade escape… Might it be Foley himself? She wasn't sure about Foley's motives, but it was clear as the California sky that he didn't care about her, not really. He'd care even less about her son, if he knew.

Thoughts spinning and stomach churning, she forced herself to breathe and pray until weariness overwhelmed her agitation and she fell asleep.

She astonished herself by not awakening until early evening. The old clock on the bedside table read just after five. Her senses whirled as she tried to put the fragments in place. She was at Roughwater Ranch, safe, for now, temporary as it was. Ben was safe with Nana Jo. The clank of dishware and the succulent smell of grilled meat drifted down the hallway.

Heaving out a breath, she smoothed her tumble of curls and headed for the kitchen to thank Aunt Ginny for the supplies.

"Well, hello there," Ginny said, hefting a bowl of steaming potatoes. "I wasn't sure if we should wake you or fix a plate for later."

"You don't need to cook for me."

She thrust the bowl into Jane's hands. "I cook for everyone, if my work allows."

"Your work?"

She laughed. "Don't look so surprised. I'm a CPA. I run an accounting firm along with carrying out my ranch duties." Her grin widened. "I confess I enjoy the expression on people's faces when I tell them that. In their imaginations, Aunt Ginny should be a quiet, demure little lady who feeds the cowpokes, tends the fire and darns socks. Well, I do that, except for the sock darning, but I also balance the books around here."

Jane smiled. "Is Uncle Gus a businessman, too?"

Ginny took up a platter and opened the side door for Gus, who was carrying a pan of grilled brisket and vegetables. He handed her the meat and leaned in to kiss her on the neck.

"Uncle Gus is a cowboy, through and through."

Gus winked at Ginny. "That's why you're crazy about me. Every girl loves a cowboy, right? You love me for my hat and spurs?"

Ginny laughed. "Among other things."

Jane felt a pang deep inside at the love that shone clear as a beacon between Gus and Ginny. She'd thought she had that with Wade. Again she scrolled rapid-fire through the misgivings, the tiny suspicions that should have told her he was not what he appeared to be.

The obsessive need to maintain his expensive Mercedes, in which there was never to be any food or drink. His compulsion to take numerous showers each day and his obsequious flattery about her looks, urging her to have her nails done, her hair professionally cut.

You have a business image to maintain, right, Janey?

She'd thought his hands-off attitude toward her fledgling floral business was his way of showing trust in her, the separation of their funds a practical attempt to sort out their finances to make their tax situation easier. She'd never suspected he was ashamed of having a wife who "peddled flowers like the village beggar," as she'd heard him say in the courtroom. He wanted his own warped image of a trophy wife, attractive, well-bred, soft-spoken, to complement his pretend real-estate career, certainly not a working-class girl.

Odd, since the women he killed were exactly that— a woman who drove her own taxi, a dental hygienist, a horse trainer and Bette Whipple, a newly minted nurse on vacation from her job in a radiology lab. Nothing outwardly remarkable about any of them, except that they were all blonde and outgoing, while Jane was brunette and quiet.

Why not you, Jane? Why didn't Wade kill you, too?

She jumped, to find Aunt Ginny touching her arm. "Are you okay? You were deep in thought for a moment there."

Jane nodded. "Yes. I…I just wanted to thank you for allowing me to stay here. I should go."

"Not until you've had dinner and a night in a warm bed."

Not until nightfall, so you can sneak away without being seen, her gut told her.

"But…" she started to say to Ginny's departing back.

Gus caught her eye. "One thing I've learned in forty years of marriage is Ginny's like the tide—she's gonna carry you along whether you like it or not. Fortunately, she's usually right about the direction. She prays a lot, so that helps her determine the course. Come on. Let's eat, then. Boys are back."

There was nothing left to do but follow Gus into the dining room.

TEN

Mitch, Chad and Liam were already seated at the table. They were scrubbed clean, but their clothes spoke of hard work on the ranch. All three stood, and, with cheeks burning, she avoided Mitch's eyes and slid into a seat next to him.

"Let's pray," Ginny said and everyone joined hands around the table while Ginny prayed. Jane found her palm swallowed up in Mitch's wide grasp. His touch was warm and strong, though she knew he was probably recoiling at the forced intimacy with her. For an unaccountable reason, her body reacted to the contact, and she realized she had not held a man's hand for a very long while. Wade had never enjoyed touching unless he initiated it, so she'd learned to keep her affectionate gestures to herself. She probably should have taken it as another warning sign, but she'd missed it, along with everything else. She found herself adding to the prayer, asking the Lord to soften Mitch's heart toward Him.

Aunt Ginny finished and everyone began to dig in to the platters of grilled green beans and peppers, brisket, and creamy mashed potatoes. As Ginny described, Gus, Mitch and Liam ate heartily while Chad's portion was smaller. Jane's mouth watered at the food, and she tried not to wolf it down, doing her best to be an invisible fly on the wall in this place she did not belong.

The conversation moved to Chad.

"Got three guys coming next month," he said quietly. "Thinking of adding Rio into the program for them to work with." He raised a questioning eyebrow at Mitch.

Mitch nodded. "Challenging horse. Great potential if he can be broke. These guys have any experience?"

"None that I know of," Chad said.

"Do they have their life insurance paid up?" Liam said around a mouthful of potatoes, earning a peeved look from Chad.

Ginny explained, "Chad's starting up a therapy program for wounded veterans, in honor of his father." Something flickered in Chad's eyes but he did not speak, so she continued. "The soldiers will come and stay at the ranch and work with some of our difficult horses, help out with the cattle, as a way to ease them back into civilian life."

"That's wonderful," Jane said.

Chad nodded. "The adjustment is brutal, for some. They're different because of their combat experience, but the world expects them to be the same people as they were before deployment."

His demeanor was of one who knew exactly how hard the transition could be. She wondered what his father had been through and where he was now.

"Mitch said you are a florist. Where is your shop, honey?" Ginny asked.

"It's... I mean, it was in Texas. I had to close up after the trial." It hurt to say it almost as much as it had pained her to walk away from her darling little shop, where she'd sweated over the tiniest detail. She missed the fragrance most of all, the spicy floral perfume that hit her senses every time she'd unlocked the door, an oasis during the last few months of her marriage, when her fears about Wade had begun to escalate. She'd found comfort among the petals, until it was all stripped away.

The awkward silence lasted until Gus put his fork down. "Excellent meal, Ginny, as usual. I can't wait for next week when you start in on pies. I'm putting in my order for cherry."

"The cooking class is starting with apple, so you'll have to hold your horses, so to speak."

He gave her a solemn nod. "I'm good at waiting, especially when there's pie in the offing."

Jane was not. As the sun sank below the sea cliffs visible through the enormous front windows, she chafed. When darkness came, she would take her leave of this sanctuary and somehow make her way to Mitch's. Then she'd get to town for a new cell phone and cash and go for her son. There was no firm destination fixed in her mind, only the deep-seated craving to hold her boy, to wrap him up tight to her chest and breathe in the scent of him, more pleasing than the perfect flower. They had to run, disappear and find somewhere else to hold on until Wade was captured.

After the dishes were washed and put away, Jane thanked Ginny again.

"We can talk in the morning about your plans," Ginny said.

Jane nodded and turned away, unwilling to lie to such a lovely woman. As she was about to let herself into the guest room, she realized Mitch was leaning against the wall in the hallway outside, arms crossed.

She jumped.

"Sorry. Didn't meant to startle you. Here." He handed her a cell phone. "Just a cheapie disposable I had Chad pick up in town. I programmed my cell in there."

She laughed. "I didn't think you knew how to use one."

He huffed out a breath. "Used plenty of technology as a marshal. I just chose not to after I got out. Figured Aunt Ginny was right considering the situation, so I took it out of the box."

She laughed. "Thank you."

He paused. "I put Foley's number in there, too, in case you change your mind."

"I won't."

"What are you going to do, then?"

She shrugged.

"Run?"

She felt a stab of irritation at his prodding. "Why do you care, Mitch? You made it clear you don't trust me, and you won't work with me to catch Wade. So what does it matter to you where I go?"

His gaze raked the floor, and he winced as if pained. "I just think it'd be hard to be on the run with a kid. He doesn't deserve that kind of life."

"Did any of us deserve what Wade did to us?" Her voice was low, but the bitterness carried clearly.

Mitch remained silent.

"Ben doesn't deserve any of the things he's had to endure, but I'm going to give him something better."

He angled a look at her then, not harsh, but inquisitive. "What if you can't?"

"God gave Ben to me for a reason." She fought through the constriction in her throat. "He is my purpose and my passion, and I will succeed with God's help. I have no future, but Ben does."

Mitch was stone still, his expression unreadable in the dim light. "That's a hard way to look at your own life…futureless."

"It's the same way you feel," she guessed. "You're going through the motions here, in your solitary cabin, but you're not living like a man who has a future, either."

Something told her she'd hit the mark.

"I'm just fine with the today part. You gotta go out on a limb to believe in tomorrow."

To believe in God, he meant. She was about to speak when he cleared his throat. "You'll be safe here until morning."

"Good night, Mitch," she said, closing the door. *I'll be gone by morning. I'll save you the trouble of going out on a limb for me.*

Mitch headed away into the darkness.

Since it was faster to get down to the rickety dock where his father lived by horse than by car, Mitch saddled Rosie, and fifty minutes later he left her to nose around the swatch of rocky sand and made his way along the weathered dock. There were only a few slips available, one taken by a boat belonging to Chad, one empty, and the farthest was home to his father's ugly thirty-four-foot trawler. The exterior was old and scabby, but somehow Pops managed to keep a wooden planter strapped to the dock as a sort of makeshift window box, full to bursting with some sort of plants Mitch couldn't identify. He called out and received an answering shout from inside the cabin. He could have made do with a phone call, but he had a strong urge to see his father in the flesh.

As he stepped into the cramped cabin, his father got up from the wooden table where he was meticulously sorting and labeling a selection of seed envelopes. His father was a few inches shorter than Mitch, but his long silver hair was still threaded with dark strands, pulled into the neat braid he'd worn his whole life. He still stood straight, black eyes as sharp as ever.

"Son," he said, hugging Mitch tightly. "Glad to see you."

A blanket on the sofa indicated his father had been napping, though the man would never admit to needing a rest. Mitch eyed the newly cut cupboard doors propped against the walls, part of the ongoing maintenance necessary for a life at sea. "Quality work."

"I don't do any other kind." Then he lapsed into silence and waited for Mitch to speak, the same way he'd always done.

"You know Wade's out."

A tightening of the mouth, a nod, his fingers toying with the seed envelopes.

"He wants me dead and to abduct his ex-wife, Jane."

Pops dropped his head then, elbows propped on his knees. "I thought it was finally over when he went to prison."

"It will be when I put him back there."

"Not the cops?"

"No. Me. Like last time. There's a marshal assigned, Al Foley, but I don't trust him. We have some history."

His father weighed that, brow creased in thought. "Liam told me that you were protecting Jane."

Mitch nodded. "She isn't a part of Wade's evil, never was."

Pops slanted a look at him and held it.

"Are you going to ask me how I know?"

Pops shook his head. "No."

"Why not?"

"It's enough that you know it. To make that reversal, after so much hatred, well, that's a God thing, and I'm not going to second-guess it."

Mitch felt suddenly weary. "How is any of this a God thing, Pops? You and Jane both. Mom's dead, your son's a serial killer and he's ready to kill again. What kind of God allows that and why would you follow Him, exactly?"

Pops massaged a shoulder with one palm. "I have two sons, and I love them both."

"Love?" He gaped outright. "You love Wade?"

"I hate what he's done, I want him punished and put away so he can't hurt anyone again, and I detest the evil in his soul, but, yes, deep down a part of me will always love my son."

"How can you? He's evil personified. How is it humanly possible that you still love him?"

Pops smiled. "It isn't. That's how I know God's in it, in my life."

The simplicity of that stopped him. His own heart was filled with such bitterness, murky hopelessness, caged by his own hatred. In that instant, he caught a glimpse of the freedom that God offered both his father and Jane. He could not love Wade, he never would, but his father's and Jane's ability to believe in God's love for everyone churned his emotions like a propeller powering a boat through stormy seas.

Pops neatly stacked a half-dozen seed packets and rubber banded them. "The human heart is wired to love, because God made it that way. That's His plan, but sometimes things go askew because of the choices we make." He rattled the envelopes. "The seeds don't take root properly—the plant gets messed up."

Messed up did not even begin to describe it. "Pops…" He broke off and stood, pacing the confines of the cabin. "I think you should come back to the ranch, in case Wade figures out where you are."

"He won't come to me, Mitch, and if he does, he won't find any aid."

"Still…the ranch is more secure."

"I've got to finish this work. I'll come back for a visit in a few days. I've got my cell phone if I need anything. Most of the time I can get a signal. Not leaving my boat."

Mitch recognized the stubborn set to his father's features, the same one he was sure shone on his own face on a regular basis. Sighing, he checked the screen on his dad's cell phone. "A satellite phone would…"

His father laughed heartily. "You know if you start preaching the benefits of carrying a fancy phone around you might be struck down by lightning for your own hypocrisy."

Mitch allowed a smile. "Yeah, I know, but I'm carrying one at the moment." He used paper and pencil from the countertop to write his number. On his way out, he pulled his father close.

Pops, I love you, he wanted to say, but he let his arms communicate what his tongue could not.

"Be safe, Pops," he breathed.

"You, too, son."

The bracing ocean air chilled him as he exited the boat. He hadn't made it off the vessel when Foley came into view, strolling along the dock. He stopped, taking in both men.

"Mr. Whitehorse," he called to Pops, ignoring Mitch,

"I'm US Marshal Al Foley. I'm tasked with capturing Wade."

Pops answered with a nod.

"Has Wade contacted you?"

"No."

"Do you have phone service here?"

"Yes, most time it works."

Foley chewed his upper lip. "Fugitives need three things…"

"Money, a means of communication and a place to stay," Mitch finished. "We know. Pops knows."

Foley shot him a look. "What I want to hear from Mr. Whitehorse is, if Wade comes looking for those things, is he going to get aid from you?"

Fury clawed up Mitch's throat like a wildcat. "You…"

Pops held up a hand; the only thing that would stop Mitch from speaking out was his father's silent command. "I will not provide any help to Wade, Marshal Foley. He's my son, yes, but I know what he is. I've known it a lot longer than you have."

Foley's gaze narrowed, shifting to Mitch, who could hardly breathe for anger. What his father had endured, the years of trying to do battle with Wade's evil, the recluse Pops had become until he found sanctuary here with his brother-in-law Gus…

"If you hear from him," Foley said, "call the local PD and they'll get hold of me immediately."

Pops didn't answer as Foley strode back down the dock, got into his car and drove away.

Mitch saw the glimmer of tears in his father's eyes as he watched. "When will it end?" he heard his father mumble as he turned back to the comfort of his boat.

As soon as I can find him, Mitch thought. *And this time he'll never hurt anyone again.*

* * *

Mitch wasn't surprised when he heard the floorboards in the entryway squeak at a tad after midnight.

"It's raining. You're gonna need a jacket," he murmured from his spot in the shadows.

Jane jumped, a low cry erupting from her mouth when she picked out his silhouette as he sat there in the darkness. Both hands went to her throat, and he felt a pang of regret for having frightened her. Jane had already experienced enough fear to last a lifetime.

He was sprawled out on an easy chair, legs crossed in front of him, singing in his head. Mitch never sang aloud, but for some reason the sappy country songs his mother used to croon had become embedded at the cellular level.

Like the river to the sea,
I never dreamed how good it could be.

Silly, maudlin, self-delusion, but nonetheless the words hummed through his soul just as strong now as they had when he was six years old. Strange for a guy who didn't have a future, only a train wreck of a past. Shoving away the thoughts, he got up and faced her.

"You scared me. What are you doing up?" she managed after a moment.

"Liam's moving a herd today. One of the horses his crew is taking has been off. I wanted to check on him. Figured I was up anyway. I don't sleep much."

She sighed. "Me neither."

"Cutting out?"

Her chin was up, but she didn't answer. He saw she had a canvas bag that Ginny had given her, the clothes she'd struggled out of the ocean in and her tattered jacket folded over her arm. He had the sudden intense urge to wrap her in a new coat, maybe green, to bring out the tiny flecks of emerald he'd spotted in her silver gaze. He blinked back to the now. "I'm thinking you're headed to wherever you got your boy hidden."

Still no answer.

"It's a long walk to anywhere, a good ten miles to town. No one about at this hour. How you gonna get there? Thinking of swiping a truck or borrowing a horse?" He supposed he'd meant some kind of joke by it, but she didn't take it that way.

"No. I don't steal things. I was going to walk to town, but I realized I forgot something at your place."

"What?"

"My pouch. It has my driver's license and ATM card. I left it in your bathroom when I took a shower."

"Okay. I'll go up and get it. You can stay, get some more sleep."

She shook her head. "I'm not coming back here. You can drop me in town after I get my pouch, or just let me out wherever it's convenient."

He frowned. "I do have some level of manners. I'll take you to town after, if that's what you want."

"Thank you."

Her gaze raked his face, but she didn't say anything further, and he had no idea what to add. Without commenting, he went to the closet and took his barn jacket from the hanger, handing it to her. "Here. You won't be warm enough in that."

Before she could protest, he escorted her out to the truck, opening the passenger door for her, which seemed to surprise her.

She tossed him a wry smile. "Do you feel like you should be putting me in the back seat in handcuffs?"

His cheeks warmed. Two days ago that was exactly what he would have thought to do with Jane Reyes, but now he was adrift. "You were not charged with any crimes," he said lamely.

She laughed. "I should put that on a résumé. I'm sure people would flock to hire me."

He climbed behind the wheel and took the road up to his cabin.

"I was afraid I'd have to ride a horse all the way up again."

He chuckled. "There's a fire road. Bumpy in some places, but serviceable. I use it sometimes if I'm not riding up and back."

"When did you come to work at the ranch?"

"After I sent Wade to jail." His brother's name seemed to taint the air. He cracked the window to allow in the cool scent of the sea. "My uncle needed a hired hand, so I bought the cabin, such as it is."

"You didn't want to live on the ranch?"

"I like my solitude."

"So I gathered. And you have no need for the modern conveniences, either."

He pretended to take offense, pointing to his belt. "Hey, I'm carrying a cell phone, aren't I?"

She laughed again. The ride grew steep and bumpy, bits of rock pinging against the chassis.

It was cold, but he welcomed the mixture of scents, the tang of the sea, the spicy aroma of eucalyptus, all fresh and bracing as if all the air in the world was birthed right here on this land. They didn't talk, except when she exclaimed over a bird that swooped silently through the night, thick bodied and tufted.

"Great horned owl," he said. "I could…" He'd almost

said *I could show you where they nest* before he caught himself. Nutty idea, but it bothered him that he'd never really wanted to show anyone else before until just now. Why now and why her, of all people?

She peered in between the gaps in the trees until they finally reached a flat graveled surface. "Gotta park here. Cabin's just over that rise."

Mitch felt the skin crawling on the back of his neck, memories of their frantic journey to the cabin after Wade nearly killed him. He'd grown comfortable with Wade in prison, more confident than a person with a serial killer for a brother had a right to. He'd begun to sink himself into life on the ranch, to accept the quiet existence tucked between the pasture and the sea.

Are you too slow-witted after your years of retirement not to see the obvious? Foley had said. *Or too complacent?*

Mitch felt again the flush of unease. Should he have insisted that Jane stay behind? Were his instincts chattering, or was it paranoia?

The cabin sat quiet and undisturbed, no fresh tire tracks or hoofprints to indicate activity. Wade would not have chosen to sit around and wait to see if Mitch returned. So why was his gut still cinched tight?

"Wait here," he said. "I'll be back."

Jane didn't question him, watching silently from the truck as he walked to the top of the rise. He listened a moment, scanning for signs of intrusion. When nothing presented itself, he strode quickly to the cabin, let himself inside and listened again. Quiet, save for water dripping off the eaves. There was sufficient moonlight for him to navigate, but he grabbed the Maglite from the clip on the wall anyway. No sense activating the generator. The old cop habit made him avoid the squeakier floorboards as he poked his head into the bedroom and kitchen. Nothing amiss, nothing moved.

Paranoia, then, he chided himself, grabbing her pouch from the bathroom and shoving it into his back pocket. He headed for the door, hesitating at the train table.

Ben loves trains.

Mitch didn't know the smallest thing about kids, but he did remember vividly his seventh birthday present, a model train his father had put together in the evenings in the garage to surprise Mitch. He'd been so excited about that train, he slept with it under his pillow. First thing every morning his fingers searched out the sleek metal lines until one time he'd woken up to find it gone. He'd surmised exactly what had happened, confronting his brother, near hysterical, but Wade only gave a wide-eyed innocent stare.

"Wade wouldn't take your train," his mother soothed.

He would do that and more. At only five years of age, Wade was already the consummate liar.

Ben would like the train, he thought. It was a startling idea, since he'd never clapped eyes on the kid, but he felt a compelling urge. He'd give it to Jane to pass on to Ben someday when he was old enough.

He went to the train table, shone the flashlight on it and stopped short. The locomotive was gone.

"Poor Mitch," came the voice, low and raspy behind him. "Did someone steal your train again?"

He did not make it completely around before Wade pressed the stun gun to his lower back. The crackle mingled with Mitch's cry of pain as the electric shock sizzled through his body. The flashlight spiraled out of his grasp as he collapsed. Shock overwhelmed his nervous system, the current carving a path of paralysis that locked his spasming muscles.

Get up, get up, his mind screamed at him, but he could not do anything but lie there in a fetal position, limbs quivering, nerves firing agony through his frame.

Enough of his senses remained intact to register the smell of gasoline, acrid and stinking, glugging from a can. He watched through blurry eyes as Wade doused the small sitting room, tossing the empty container on the rocking chair.

"Mitch," Wade said, backtracking to the kitchen. "I expected more from you. You hardly put up more of a fight than the women. I fantasized every single day in prison how I would kill you, but this is hardly even satisfying." He sounded as if he was a man discussing a mediocre play he'd just attended.

"Y-you…" Mitch stammered.

"What's that?" Wade arched a palm around his ear. "Are you begging or apologizing? I can't tell."

"You belong in a cage," Mitch spit, forcing the words through the wall of pain.

Wade smiled and flicked a small cigarette lighter to life. The orange flame danced double in Mitch's compromised vision.

"I'll never be put in a cage again, Mitch." He laughed. "It's dark in here, big brother. Let me add some light, shall I?"

Almost in slow motion, Wade dropped the lighter, the gasoline vapors igniting before it hit the floor.

ELEVEN

Jane sat in the passenger seat, twiddling her new cell phone, eyes trained on the spot where Mitch had disappeared. Seconds ticked into minutes—five, ten, fifteen. The darkness closed around her like a fist. Her skin was chilled and she wanted to roll up the window, but Mitch had taken the keys. Pewter fog ribboned the sky.

She began to shiver. An awful thought drifted through her mind—what if something had happened and Mitch did not return?

"Stop it," she told herself. "You've been taking care of yourself all this time. You don't need to panic because you're left alone for a few minutes." Something drifted on the breeze, a strange, pungent whiff that she could not place at first.

When the anxiety refused to be quieted, she got out and crept to the top of the rise. The hollow below was ink black, the house silhouetted by the moonlight that shone through the fog, windows dark. Mitch had not started the generator, it seemed, but that was not surprising. He would only be there long enough to retrieve her pouch. But why was it taking so long? Before she could talk herself out of it, she tapped out a text.

Everything okay?

The wind rattled the leaves in the scruffy bushes as she waited for a reply that didn't come. Perhaps Mitch hadn't noticed the text. A rustling in the grass indicated the night creatures were on the prowl.

She waited until the odor quivered her nostrils again. Burning, it was the smell of something burning. Electrified, her eyes went wide, lungs caught in midbreath. A flicker of orange showed around the edges of the closed curtains. Her stomach dropped to her shoes.

Fire! While her nerves shouted at her to sprint to the cabin and help Mitch, doubt assailed her from all sides. What if it was a trap? It had to be. Wade was waiting for her, for Mitch. She should call for help. Her cell phone screen taunted her with the message...no service.

She could text Marshal Foley, but what could he do? She tapped the message anyway. Fire at Mitch White-horse's cabin. Send help. There was no solace in the sending, since she knew if Mitch was inside he would be dead before any kind of help arrived.

Oh, Lord, she prayed. *What should I do?*

It was sheer lunacy to run into a burning building, especially since she knew deep down the fire had to be Wade's handiwork. But how could she let Mitch die without lifting a finger? Mitch would be another victim of Wade's monstrous evil. Her ignorance had cost three women their lives, but this was unfolding right in front of her, the flames now showing bigger and the smell of burning wood assaulting her senses as the fire began to gobble up the old cabin. Her body told her to run, but her heart did not consent.

Jane Reyes had been many things—foolish, naive,

clueless and needy—but she was not going to add coward to the list. She wouldn't let Mitch burn to death, not
if it was in her power to save him.

Before fear changed her feet to stone, she pocketed
her phone and sprinted down the slope toward the burning cabin. Skidding on wet grass, she slipped and slid
her way down the hill and onto the gravel path, nearing
the front door. Smoke was thickening, swirling around
the edges of the curtain and under the doorjamb. As she
neared, some of the wood shingles ignited with a pop
that made her jump.

"Mitch," she shouted as she closed the gap. "Mitch,
can you hear me?"

Raising a hand to push the door open, she was pulled
backward by the hood of her jacket. She stumbled, fell
and found herself staring up into the face of Wade Whitehorse. Time stopped, the fire receded in her mind and
all that was left was pure, undiluted terror.

The moonlight painted his skin in bland luminos-
ity that almost blended with the white of his teeth. He
wore jeans and a denim jacket, the perfect imitation of
a country cowboy. A friendly, charming serial killer.
"Hello, Janey," he said. "You're here just in time. You
were always so prompt for everything."

Trapped in a nightmare from which she could not
awaken, her body began to tremble. He regarded her
with a wide smile. "You look nice. You've grown your
hair out. I like it, though the bangs need a trim."

Stall him, her instincts screamed. Foley would send
help. *Just keep him talking.* It was not easy to force her
mouth to make syllables, but she managed. "T-time for
what?"

"In time to watch Mitch die." Wade said it with a

smile, nodding in that way that meant he was pleased with his own cleverness.

"No, Wade." It came out as a whisper.

He shot a quizzical look at her. "You know, I wondered, I mean, I really puzzled over why you came here to the coast. I tracked you to your rented room, but you'd already gone—come here, I later found out. But why? That was the question that tormented me. Why would you go to my brother, the man who sent your husband to prison?"

She found she could not answer, propped up on her elbows, staring at him while another shingle erupted into flame with a shrill hiss.

He snapped his fingers. "Then it came to me." His smile was coy. "You knew, didn't you, Janey?"

She tried twice before the sound came out. "Knew what?"

"Where I would go." He sounded so pleased, she could only gape at him as he continued. "As soon as you heard of my escape, you came here, to Mitch, because you knew I'd head right on over to kill him." The words were infused with such friendly cheer he might have been speaking of attending the neighborhood block party. "You'd be sure to find me, wouldn't you? Clever wifey."

Delusional, insane. "We're divorced, Wade. I'm not your wife anymore."

He aimed a kindly smile, crouched next to her and reached to pat her knee, stopping just before he made contact. She had to force herself not to recoil.

"The divorce was the most practical decision at the time, and I want you to know I don't fault you for it, not in the least. It doesn't matter what the courts or anybody else says, anyway, Janey. You'll always be mine."

Something stone cold slithered up her back and clutched tight around her throat. She found herself pushing out the words as if she was expelling poison from her gut, voicing the question that had plagued her from the beginning. "You killed those women, Wade. Why? Why am I different? Why didn't you kill me, too?"

He sighed, cocking his head, birdlike. "Silly Janey. You're my wife. I selected you because you're the most suitable. Pretty, intelligent, easygoing, trusting, affectionate—though that was annoying sometimes. Minimal family ties. You are the one I chose and groomed, not like the others. They were just means to an end, not quality like you, Janey." He pointed to his heart. "You're my wife forever. We are going to go where they can't find us." He winked at her. "I think it's about time we started a family, don't you?"

Started a family. So he didn't know about Ben. A sliver of relief stabbed through the terror, the tiniest pinprick of hope. Her son was still safe. She got to her feet, feeling the heat on her neck. The crackling of the roof shingles swelled ominously. Wade stood and surveyed the growing inferno with satisfaction.

Jane swallowed, throat parched. "You can't let him burn to death, Wade."

He blinked as if the thought startled him. "Why not?"

"Because..." She groped for an idea. "They'll find you. The marshals are looking all over. Someone must have called in the smoke. They're probably already on their way to arrest you."

He laughed. "Oh, trust me, the marshals won't be a problem, but I appreciate your concern. Leave all the details to me, Janey." He crooked a finger at her. "Come on. Let's go."

"Where?"

A flash of annoyance crossed his brow. "I explained that already. The location isn't important." He gazed up at the sky and frowned. "I feel like it might start to rain soon, and you know I don't like being wet." He gestured impatiently. "Now, Janey."

She could run, sprint out into the trees or back to the truck. Her legs were paralyzed with fear as he moved closer.

"We're going now," he said again, a placid smile on his face. "Mitch is already dead. He put me in prison, and now he's dead, so justice has been served and we can move on."

"Just let me check, Wade," she said. "To be sure he's dead."

"No need, my sweet."

But she already had her palm on the door.

"No, Janey," he said, voice steely now. "I don't want you smelling of smoke."

In the distance came the whine of sirens. Wade jerked a look toward the fire trail as headlights probed the trees.

At the same moment, the glass shattered in the front window and Jane ducked reflexively, covering her face. Wade reached for her, his fingertips grazing her sleeve as a rifle appeared through the broken glass.

Mitch caught the barest glimpse of Jane through the smoke. He fired high with the first shot, clear of Jane with an extra margin of safety built in. She screamed low and to his right. Wade returned fire. The bullets shattered the remaining glass and took a chunk out of the window frame.

"Stay down, Jane," he shouted, but there was little chance she heard him over the bullets and the crackling fire. The changing angle of Wade's shots indicated he'd moved, taken cover, probably, behind the woodpile. He risked another quick poke and a volley of shots. Nerves rattling, he yanked the front door open.

Jane was crouched on the porch in a ball, arms covering herself. There was no time to go about it in a gentle manner, so he simply picked her up and ran back into the cabin, bullets slamming into the closing door. He released her and she instinctively started to leap to her feet, but he pulled her down by one wrist under the safety of the window frame.

"You hit?"

She shook her head. "I think you both managed to miss me."

The wry humor was so incongruous with the circumstances that he actually smiled for a moment.

"Keep low," he said. He figured he must be quite a sight, covered in black soot, sweating all over and muscles still spasming from the effects of the stun gun.

Her eyes were wide in the gloom as their situation slowly dawned on her. The kitchen was fully engulfed in fire, cutting off their exit to the rear. The flames were slowly marching toward the living room.

Wade's voice carried over the fire. "You gotta come out, Mitch, or burn to death in there. Send Janey—you don't want her to die with you, right? The big, bad marshal wouldn't sentence an innocent to death? Only your brother. Isn't that right, Mitch?"

Mitch looked at Jane.

"I texted Foley," she said. "The police are close. I can hear the sirens."

He nodded. They needed time, minutes maybe. He gripped his rifle, fighting the urge to suck in a deep breath of the poisoned air. "Got an idea, but it's not guaranteed."

"Anything." It was only one word, but the strength of it, the trust in it, trust in him, robbed him of speech. She would rather put her life in Mitch's risky plan than go back to Wade. In that moment, he knew he'd misjudged her completely. She'd never been a part of Wade's plans. Jane Reyes was Wade's victim just as much as anyone. After a slow nod, he fired out the window, then grabbed her hand, drawing them stumbling toward the closet. Inside he yanked up the trapdoor and guided her to the ladder.

"Cellar. Go."

She didn't pause, just did as he directed. As soon as she cleared the ladder, he followed, drawing the trapdoor closed and swinging the latch into place to lock it from the inside. Flimsy—it was intended to secure the house from bears who managed to infiltrate the cellar, but it would slow Wade down, he hoped.

The cellar was no more than a ten-by-ten space, cold and dark. The earth that surrounded the structure kept the walls perpetually moist, the cement floor frigid, and allowed for the occasional tunneling rodent. Even in the heat of summer, Mitch found it too cold for more than a quick visit.

Jane flicked a light to life on her phone, shining it around the space. Crude wooden shelves held jars of strawberry jelly and a big glass container of some dark, mysterious liquid that had been here when he bought the old place.

He went immediately up the far steps, which sloped up to the heavy wood door. "Exits to the woods behind the cabin. We can…" Her scream startled him, and he whirled around.

Her hand was holding the phone light, which trembled in her grasp, illuminating a dirty animal cowering in the corner. He heard her relieved exhalation. "It's a cat, I think. Somehow it found a way in." Like Wade would do soon enough. "This place has more holes than a golf course. We have to get out."

The cat mewled plaintively—a kitten, really, no bigger than his palm. He paid minimal attention, his mind spinning out the possible scenarios. Stay put, and they'd be safe from the fire for a while and perhaps Wade wouldn't know where they'd gone. Or exit into the woods, also safe from the fire, but exposed for a time until they made it to the tree line.

"Stay or go?" he said, as much to himself as her.

She was crouched down, reaching for the little cat. "I say we stay. Wade won't come in the house. Too much smoke. He won't know about the cellar, right?"

The beam of light caught her tapered fingers, caressing the tiny mewling creature. The mewing was lost in a cacophonous sound. Jane bolted to her feet.

"What was that?"

The heavy wooden door shuddered under the weight of another blow.

Mitch's throat went dry. "It's my ax. He took it from the woodpile. He's cutting his way in."

They listened to the sound of the blade punching through the last barrier between them.

TWELVE

Jane watched in horror as a piece of wood broke loose from the door and tumbled down the steps to land at Mitch's feet. He was already running to the ladder, but he was back in a moment, face grim. "Trapdoor is hot to the touch. We can't get out that way."

"Mitch." Wade's voice was oddly muffled. "I didn't think you were a coward, hiding behind my wife. Let her out now and I'll kill you quickly. I don't want her damaged."

Damaged, as if she was a piece of pottery or a computer part. Damaged? Oh yes, she was certainly that, but the broken pieces had been glued together, thanks to God, and as long as she had Ben, she'd never be ripped apart again.

"Give it up, Wade. Cops are on their way," Mitch shouted. His words were lost in the rapid blows of the ax biting into the wood.

"I'm coming, Janey," Wade yelled. "Don't you let him touch you." A hole appeared in the middle of the door as another hunk fell away.

To combat the surge of helplessness, she grabbed a flat shovel from the spot under the cupboard. The movement startled the kitten, who leaped up onto the high shelf. Mitch had the rifle ready.

"Squeeze behind the shelves, if you can," he said.

She shook her head. "I'm going to help you if he breaks through."

"This is a tight space, and the bullets are going to fly. Protect yourself."

"He won't win." She gripped the shovel, shoulders squared with a will of iron, though her body felt brittle as glass. "I won't let him."

Mitch's face was streaked with sweat, eyes tar black. "You have a son. Staying alive, that's all that matters."

Being with Wade isn't living, she wanted to say. *It's a death sentence.*

Another hunk of wood fell through near the tarnished knob. Now Wade's gun barrel poked through the hole, and she watched in some sort of slow-motion terror as his finger pressed the trigger. The bullet smashed into a jar of jelly, sending shards of ooze-covered glass raining down. The scream stuck in her throat.

"You're gonna hurt Jane," Mitch thundered. "That's not what you want, is it?"

"She's mine or she's dead," Wade spit.

A wave of nausea sickened her. *Mine or dead.* Wade fired another blind round, which buried itself into the wall.

Mitch went to her, grabbed the shovel and pushed her toward the space behind the shelves. She didn't understand at first, until she saw the hole down low, a boarded-up opening where the walls had failed, scratched away by animals eager for shelter. It was the way the cat must have gotten in.

She bent down to look. The opening, no more than three feet square, bathed her in cool air. Mitch saw it, too.

"Pull the boards away. You can squeeze out."

"No."

The ax split through the door. Wade pulled it free and hacked again.

Mitch put his hand on the small of her back, but she resisted. "Just…please," he said.

He was asking. She'd not heard him ask for anything from her, just issue orders. Now he gave her a pained look that she couldn't decipher, as if he was about to ingest poison, and then called to Wade. "All right. You win. I'll open the door."

Jane shook her head violently, grabbing at his wrist. "No, Mitch," she breathed.

His face was inches from hers. "You have to live."

"Not this way."

"You'll have a chance to escape."

"He'll kill you."

"He'll try, and while he's busy about it, you run. Hard. Lose him in the woods."

"No," she hissed.

He exhaled long and slow and then touched her face with the calloused fingers of his left hand. "Please," he said again.

How was it possible that Mitch Whitehorse was offering up his safety as a security for hers? In wonder, she reached up and put her hand over his. It seemed to surprise him, but just for a moment, he relaxed a fraction into the touch, and something ever so subtly gentled in his eyes. Then he took her palm away and pulled her toward the hole. Uncertain, she was struggling with whether to resist or comply when her phone buzzed. She'd forgotten it was still in her pocket. The soft glow illuminated the text.

"It's Foley," she whispered in Mitch's ear. "He's closing in right now."

He considered a moment.

"Stay low, crawl into the hole." He took up the rifle and sneaked to the other side of the space. At first she didn't know why he began firing at the hole in the door when it was clear his bullets would not penetrate the thick wood. Wade returned fire through the spot he'd carved out, aiming now for Mitch's location, next to another shelf of jars. Mitch was drawing Wade's fire, hoping to distract him long enough for the marshal to arrive. Wade's bullets exploded the jars. They tumbled from the shelves and rained their contents down onto the floor. She clapped her hands over her ears to block out the deafening noise. A scream built up in her throat, and just as it bubbled from her lips the shooting stopped.

There was the sound of shots again, but this time not aimed into the cellar. Police? Fire? All that mattered to her hammering heart and quivering eardrums was that the shooting had stopped. When her phone buzzed, she answered it, holding it so Mitch could hear.

"This is Danny Patron of the Driftwood Police Department. We're outside. Wade's fled on foot, but we have eyes on him. Please exit immediately."

With a heart brimming over with relief, she tried to get her legs to comply.

While Mitch helped Jane pick her way over the glass, an officer shouted through the mangled door. "Police," he said. "Open up."

Mitch unlocked it, and the smell of smoke assailed them. He took Jane's forearm and urged her through the opening.

"But the kitten…" she said.

"Go," he insisted, pushing her through.

Officer Patron huffed out a breath. His thatch of red hair gleamed oddly metallic in the smoke-heavy air. "Come on, Mitch."

"You've got eyes on Wade?"

"Foley's tracking him. Appears he's heading for the main road. Working on a roadblock. We have to move away from the structure now."

The structure—his home, as much as he had one— was done for. He knew without visual confirmation that it was a complete loss. No matter how much water the volunteer fire department pumped on the old place, it was not going to be salvageable.

Jane followed Patron toward the strobing lights of his police car. Before Mitch trailed them out, he surveyed the wreck of the cellar, the smell of smoke now mingling with the fruity fragrance from the ruined jams. Despair slumped his shoulders and made breathing an effort. Countless hours had gone into putting up those berries, but what right had he, anyway, to set aside such things to enjoy in the future? He had no future, only a past from which he could not escape and a tomorrow in which nothing else mattered but finding his brother.

Not quite. The odd thought pricked through the desolation. Now Jane mattered, her life, her son, her freedom. Jane mattered. He wasn't sure why that warmed something inside him, but it did.

Another jar fell and shattered, jerking him away from the notion. Wade was at large, still. He had to make sure that knowledge eclipsed every other thought or feeling that rambled through him.

He was about to leave when he noticed the kitten sitting on the top shelf, shivering. He picked it up gently, and the poor shocked animal went limp in his arms, bones as fragile as straw, fur matted with jelly or blood, he wasn't sure.

Why take the cat? The scrawny thing was malnourished, judging from the size, perhaps would not even survive until the morning.

Why take the cat? Because it mattered to Jane, his heart told him unexpectedly. That thought froze him in place, cradling the fragile creature, standing in a pile of ruined glass. Why did he care what mattered to Jane?

He turned the thought this way and that in his mind until a wisp of smoke infiltrated the space and brought him back to reality. Carefully, he tucked the kitten inside his jacket and let himself out into the night.

Jane tried to gather her composure, sitting in the back seat of the police car that carried her to the Driftwood police station. She yearned to turn around, stare out the window, peer into the gloom to spot Mitch, but he had stayed with another officer, watching his cabin burn to cinders. The reality of her circumstances almost rendered her immobile. Wade wanted her back or, barring that, wanted her dead. She was not sure which was the worse alternative.

She squeezed her palms together. "Thank You, Lord, that he doesn't know about Ben." Patron led her to a chair, giving her a sweat jacket to drape over her shivering shoulders.

"My wife's," he said, "but I don't think she'd mind. She leaves an extra wherever she goes. We practically buy them by the dozens." He pressed a disposable cup

"4 for 4" MINI-SURVEY

We are prepared to **REWARD** you with 4 FREE books and Free Gifts for completing our MINI SURVEY!

Romance

Suspense

You'll get up to...

4 FREE BOOKS & FREE GIFTS

FREE
Value Over
$20!

...ust for participating in our Mini Survey!

Get Up To 4 Free Books!

Dear Reader,

IT'S A FACT: if you answer 4 quick questions, we'll send you 4 FREE REWARDS from each series you try!

Try **Love Inspired® Romance Larger-Print** books featuring Christian characters facing modern-day challenges.

Try **Love Inspired® Suspense Larger-Print** novels featuring Christian characters facing challenges to their faith... and lives

Or **TRY BOTH!**

I'm not kidding you. As a leading publisher of women's fiction, we value your opinions... and your time. That's why we are prepared to reward you handsomely for completing our mini-survey. In fact, we have 4 Free Rewards for you, including 2 free books and 2 free gifts from each series you try!

Thank you for participating in our survey,

Pam Powers

To get your 4 FREE REWARDS:
Complete the survey below and return the insert today to receive up to 4 FREE BOOKS and FREE GIFTS guaranteed!

"4 for 4" MINI-SURVEY

1 Is reading one of your favorite hobbies?
☐ YES ☐ NO

2 Do you prefer to read instead of watch TV?
☐ YES ☐ NO

3 Do you read newspapers and magazines?
☐ YES ☐ NO

4 Do you enjoy trying new book series with FREE BOOKS?
☐ YES ☐ NO

Please send me my Free Rewards, consisting of **2 Free Books from each series I select** and **Free Mystery Gifts**. I understand that I am under no obligation to buy anything, as explained on the back of this card.

❑ **Love Inspired® Romance Larger-Print** (122/322 IDL GNPV)
❑ **Love Inspired® Suspense Larger-Print** (107/307 IDL GNPV)
❑ **Try Both** (122/322/107/307 IDL GNP7)

FIRST NAME	LAST NAME

ADDRESS

APT.#	CITY

STATE/PROV.	ZIP/POSTAL CODE

READER SERVICE—Here's how it works:

filled with steaming coffee in her hands. "It's terrible stuff, like motor oil, but it's warm."

The brew made her wince when she sipped it.

"Motor oil?" he said.

"Motor oil with a side of creamer."

He laughed, settling into his chair behind the cluttered desk. A silver frame showed a picture of Patron, his wife and three little girls clustered around their knees, grinning. Each of them wore Mickey Mouse ears.

"Disneyland," he said. "Still paying the bills from that vacation."

How she craved the freedom to take Ben to Disneyland someday, carefree, not looking over her shoulder, enjoying a normal life with her son.

"Mitch and Foley are on their way."

"They… There's no news?"

He drummed his fingers on the desktop. "Not yet."

She wanted to press but didn't.

He quirked a smile. "I've been deputized by Foley as an official US marshal. First time in my career that's happened. Never been part of a federal manhunt, either. We just don't get that kind of excitement in sleepy little Driftwood."

"You make that sound like a bad thing. I'd be happy living out my life in a quiet little town with zero excitement."

He nodded, added a packet of sugar to his coffee and offered her one. "So, you should know that this… situation has drawn attention."

Dread cascaded through her nerves. She knew before she even asked. "Reporters?"

He nodded. "Woman called this afternoon, asking about Wade. Her last name is Barber, Elaine Barber.

Somehow she managed to find out that Mitch lived in town. Asked for contact info, which I did not provide, since I know Mitch will welcome an interview about as much as a root canal."

She sighed. "Yeah. Talking isn't big on his list."

"Cops and reporters, it's like…" He stopped. "I was going to say gasoline and matches, but that seems in poor taste, considering."

She held her breath, sensing there was more coming.

"This Elaine Barber also asked if you were in town."

"Me? How could she possibly know that already?"

"Beats me."

The information burned a trail along with the acid of the coffee. They would come, hunting for a story, expose her to yet another community ready to despise her—and they'd reveal Ben.

"Hey," he said.

She blinked, realizing she was clutching the arm of the chair like it was the pull cord on a parachute. "What?"

"I told them nothing."

She let out a shaky breath. "Thank you."

He shrugged. "Like I said, cops and reporters are like gasoline and matches. We don't play well together." He reached into his desk drawer. "There was one other call from a second woman."

"Another reporter?"

"She didn't come off that way. She sounded troubled, desperate, if you want my honest opinion. She said she had to talk to you, that it was urgent." He handed her a yellow paper with a phone number scrawled on it.

"Did she leave her name?"

"No." He cocked his head. "She just said to tell you that she is number four."

Jane dropped the coffee cup, a dark lake spreading across the floor under her feet. Patron fetched a roll of paper towels, and together they sopped up the mess. The coffee was probably hot to the touch, but she could not feel it, could not feel anything in the wake of those words.

Number four.

There was only one woman who would have identified herself that way.

Bette Whipple.

The fourth victim, the only woman who escaped Wade's death sentence.

THIRTEEN

There was no reason to stay and watch the volunteer firefighters work on dousing the flames. The best they could do was set up a perimeter and make sure the fire did not spread after devouring Mitch's cabin. There was nothing much of monetary value in the structure. He would miss the rocking chair his father had made for his mother, and the old mantel clock, but most of all he'd miss his trains. He'd never reveal that fact, even under pain of death, but Wade would know. Wade had always known how best to hurt those around him.

I'll never be put in a cage again, Mitch. It wasn't a threat as much as a promise, his second, delivered through the hacked edges of a solid wood door. The first quivered in his gut like a spear driven deep.

She will be mine or she will die.

As he drove the truck to the police station, the words thumped again and again inside him. What if Jane was right and the only way out was to stand and capture him together?

The cop side of him balked. It was not logical. Mitch had no badge anymore. Foley and the marshals could provide organized protection and track Wade. It was what the marshals were created for, their mission since George Washington made it so in 1789. And the marshals were the best at what they did; he knew that firsthand. Accepting their protection was the wisest course of action.

The kitten stirred against his stomach, soothed by the warmth, he imagined. He had no idea what he was going to do with a cat, and he had no brain space to worry about it. Foley's voice via the cell phone had not been encouraging, so he suspected Wade had eluded capture.

Then again, Foley might be playing with him, spooling out the drama until he could tell Mitch personally that he'd arrested Wade in spite of Jane's unwillingness to take Foley's advice and go into protective custody. Foley would relish the chance to tell Mitch he'd made the bust, taken care of a problem Mitch should have addressed decades before Wade's serial killings.

He's your brother, your kin, your burden, and you left it to others to deal with. That would be the unspoken accusation, which Mitch could not deny, since it was the same one Mitch leveled at himself.

Mitch had been a ruthlessly effective marshal, his tenacity in tracking fugitives unrivaled. There were days, weeks even, when he had lived on a few hours of sleep and forgotten to eat while on the trail of a killer. "You're a monster," the sister of a fugitive he'd tracked had shouted at him. A monster, like his brother? Two sides of a deadly coin, the cop and the killer. He put every shred of energy into his job, perhaps to prove to himself on which side of that coin he belonged.

Yet he had not tracked his brother. Mitch, the relentless marshal, had left the bomb to go off on its own, stepping in only after it had come out that Wade had killed three women, almost a fourth. Why had he buried his head in the sand? It should have been his responsibility more than anyone's to know what his brother was up to, to snuff out the fuse before it triggered the explosion.

But he hadn't. He'd walled off that part of his life, his heart, his consciousness—to maintain his own sanity, he'd told himself. But his selfishness had come at a high price.

God forgives, his father said, and Aunt Ginny concurred.

But Mitch would put no stock in that. If this God his father knew had made Wade, then Mitch wanted no part of any of it. There was life and there was death, and the whys and wherefores he'd leave to the philosophers.

As Mitch climbed out of the truck at the police station, the kitten turned around and kneaded his stomach with tiny paws. Mitch unbuttoned his flannel shirt and tucked the animal in. The kitten let out a soft mew and settled into stillness. The fragility of the living thing nestled next to his heart brought him back to a long-ago memory of his days with Paige Lynn, when he'd tried to rescue a fallen baby bird, tumbled from a nest above her porch light.

He'd held the gaping, awkward thing while she tried to administer drops of water to the parched pink throat, afraid his big fingers would damage the wobbly neck. Finally he'd noticed her smiling at him, a glorious, joyful smile that made his insides lurch.

You're such a big bear of a guy, your emotions all locked up, but sometimes you let your tender side show.

Sometimes, with her, he'd remembered he had a tender side, but when Wade had driven her away, he'd become that wild bear again, the immovable mountain with a feral heart instead of a human one. For the first time in a very long while, the thought pained him.

When the kitten was once again settled, he strode

into the police station. Foley stood, arms crossed, legs apart—cop stance.

Danny Patron was sitting at his desk, fingers twiddling. His hair stood up in red thatches from his habit of raking his hands through it. Jane was sort of wandering in directionless circles, arms wrapped around herself. She went to him when he entered.

"I'm so sorry about your cabin," she said, and he was surprised to see the gleam of tears in her eyes.

"Just a building," he said.

"What did you think was going to happen?" Foley snapped. "Wade was staking out your cabin, and you come waltzing in with his wife."

"Ex-wife," Jane said through gritted teeth.

"This isn't her fault," Mitch said. "What happened to the search?"

"I lost him."

"How?"

"He had a vehicle, a stolen car—he got enough ahead of me and ditched it. Took off on foot."

"What about dogs?"

"Closest dog is in Copper Top," Danny said. "I called. They're coming in, but my guess is he'll have doubled back to town, stolen another car."

"Why don't you have a team in place yet?" Mitch demanded. A fugitive apprehension team should have been mobilized, fanned out over the area, watching bus stations, highways, all routes of escape.

"Who says I don't?"

"I do. You lost him because you don't have backup."

Foley's eyes blazed. "You don't get to tell me how to do my job, Whitehorse. You're not a cop anymore. You're just the kinfolk of a killer."

The statement ripped the air like an obscenity. Mitch lurched forward and so did Foley until Danny stepped between them, one palm on each of their heaving chests. "Fellas, we all want the same thing here."

Mitch wasn't so sure. He saw something carved into Foley's expression, something he did not trust. Why was there no task force in place? Had Wade escaped, or had Foley let him go?

Foley stared a moment longer before turning to Danny. "I need to go over some details with you." He shot a look at Mitch. "Official details. Not for public consumption."

Danny gestured to a room behind his office. "We can talk in there."

"I'll be right back," Foley said to Jane. "Think about what just happened. Your best chance to stay alive, maybe your only chance, is to let me take you into protective custody."

He followed Danny into the back room. They closed the door.

Jane was standing hesitantly, bereft. She was not crying, but her mouth was pinched with fatigue, and she was slightly bent from the waist as if she'd been punched in the gut. Was she thinking of Ben? Wondering if Wade had somehow discerned where she was hiding him?

What could he offer her in the way of hope? Wade was still at large and he'd nearly killed them both, again. He felt acutely the loss of his badge, powerless. While he searched for words, the kitten stirred. He extracted the tiny animal from his jacket and handed it to her.

She started, taking the kitten and examining him carefully, before turning wondering silver eyes back on him. "You took him from the cellar?"

He nodded.

"I...I didn't think you'd be the kind to rescue a kitten."

He blew out a breath. "Me neither."

"Why did you?"

Because I knew it would please you. There it was again, that pesky instinct to care about what she needed. He coughed and scoured a hand over his chin. That was some kind of insane notion, which needed to be discarded immediately. "Didn't seem right to leave it there," he finally settled on.

She smiled, and something about it poked through the darkness in his soul, shining the faintest glimmer of light into his misery. He yanked his shirt smooth in an effort to do the same with his thoughts.

She reached up on tiptoe. Instinctively he bent to close the gap and she pressed a kiss to his cheek, just below the scar. "Thank you for saving the kitten," she said.

He shrugged, cleared his throat, straightened his belt. "We can take it back to the ranch. Aunt Ginny will know how to handle it."

Her expression clouded, the joy falling away, her voice a whisper. "I have to get Ben and run."

Mitch shook his head. "He'll find you. He knows you're close, and he's going to circle like a vulture until he catches your trail and learns about Ben."

"What choice do I have? And don't tell me to go with Foley, because I know you don't trust him any more than I do."

He didn't ask her how she knew. "There's bad blood between us. He has reasons for his feelings, some valid ones. I have no evidence that he's a bad cop."

She sniffed, cuddling the kitten. "I've never met a cop who trusted me, believed me..." Her gaze wandered to his face. "Including you."

The room went quiet save for the slow drip of the coffee machine. The hush seemed to squeeze the confession out of him before he made the conscious decision to speak. "I…I was wrong. I know now you weren't Wade's accomplice."

She bent her head to the kitten, stroking her cheek across his pink-tipped ears. He thought he'd said something offensive as the silence stretched on until he heard her shuddering breath and the sniffles that followed.

He didn't think then, just let his arms bring her close, folding her and the kitten gently to his chest.

"I think that's the nicest thing anyone has said to me in years," she mumbled into his shirtfront. "Thank you for believing me."

He found himself rubbing little circles into her back, as though his hands acted without consent of his mind, his need to make physical contact with her inexplicable and irresistible. She was so small and delicate, fragile, like the kitten, but with something so much stronger threading through her soul.

"What am I going to do?" Her voice broke on the last word.

"You could stay at the ranch, hidden."

She shook her head, and he let his fingers trail away as she stepped back, rubbing a free hand over her wet cheeks. "I have to get Ben. He's all that matters."

"So hide here in Driftwood. If you run, he'll know it—he has help in this town, I think. I'll get him to come to me. He wants to anyway. I'll take him down. I did it before."

The look she turned on him was shocked and tender. "You'd…you'd help me catch him?"

"Not help you—hide you." His tone went hard and flat. "I don't need your help to catch him."

"But you think I shouldn't go with Foley?"

He thought that over for a long moment. "I don't know, Jane, but my instincts say he's not telling us the complete truth."

"Maybe your instincts should be good enough for me." Her lower lip trembled. "I can't trust my own anymore."

She rested her head softly on the kitten until he could not resist. He crooked a finger under her chin and tipped her face to look at his. "Your instincts are to protect your son. You've done well at it so far."

"God's taken care of us—it wasn't my skill."

He sighed and stepped away. "Sure."

"You don't believe in God?"

"Oh, Aunt Ginny's tried her best, but I see no proof around here of God's goodness."

He was surprised when she laughed.

"Something funny?"

She held up the kitten. "You saved a kitten, so I choose to see God's goodness in you."

He grimaced. "That's a mistake. You won't find any more. If I was good, I would have tracked Wade, stayed on his trail, and those women wouldn't have died. I didn't, because I wanted to be free of him. I wanted it to be somebody else's problem. That isn't goodness. It's selfishness."

She stilled. "Your past doesn't define you, Mitch. Your God does."

He blinked, scrolling through a score of thoughts. "He's not my God, and frankly, I can't understand how He can be yours, after what's happened to you."

Those metallic eyes regarded him with a calm she had no right to, it seemed to him.

"God is the only thing in this whole wide world that cannot be taken away from me," she said.

Another inexplicable sentiment from a woman who perplexed and confounded him.

After a moment, she pulled a paper from the back pocket of her jeans. "I need to tell you something."

The door jerked open, and Foley came out. Jane put the paper back in her pocket.

"I've got a safe house ready," Foley said. "You just need to say yes. You have to trust me."

Mitch didn't say anything as Jane's eyes shifted from Foley to him and back again.

She was weighing her decision. *Go with Foley.* It was the most logical, reasonable way to protect herself and her son.

Or ally herself with Mitch, bank on keeping herself hidden and trust that Mitch would once again put the biggest evil in her life behind bars.

She would be smart to choose Foley, of course, and he didn't blame her. Once Foley arranged for protection, Mitch would probably not see her again. He looked down at his boots.

Jane Reyes deserved protection, and she would get it with Foley. He had nothing to offer her but more empty promises.

"No, thank you," he heard her say to Foley.

Mitch jerked his head up and found her looking full on at him, head cocked as if she was seeing him for the first time. Then she walked toward the door.

"Where are you going?" Foley asked.

She did not even shoot him a look over her shoulder. "I need to take care of my cat," she called as she left.

FOURTEEN

Jane could only make her body follow one direction at a time. "Get into Mitch's truck," she told herself. The jolt of cold air gave her just enough energy to make it. He joined her after a few moments, starting the engine without a word.

They drove a half mile or so before he brought the truck to a stop and cleared his throat. "I…I'm not sure this is the right timing, but I wanted to…" He looked at the night sky and then at the steering wheel. "I mean… like I said back there, I judged you wrongly. I understand now that you were Wade's victim, not his ally, so I want to say I'm sorry."

She swallowed hard. "Thank you, but you don't need to apologize. You never did me any harm."

"I heaped plenty of hate on you when you didn't deserve it." He offered a wry smile. "I figure that rates a sin in your book."

"It's your book, too, even though you don't read it."

"I read it plenty in my lifetime, looking for something— answers, I guess—but I never found anything in there that could take away from the mess."

"'Nor height, nor depth, nor any other creature, shall

be able to separate us from the love of God.' That's what I found there, Mitch, a pure love that lasts."

"My problem with that…" He sighed. "Aw, never mind. Not the right time."

"No better time," she prompted.

"Well, if you believe that, then the same applies to Wade, doesn't it? If nothing separates him from God, then there's no justice. Wade doesn't deserve the same kind of love. He's evil—that's the bottom line."

"God invites everyone, even Wade, but He doesn't compel anyone to take the invitation." She looked at Mitch. "So Wade has declined…and so have you."

He frowned. "My choice."

"Yes." She stroked the kitten, feeling the vibration of his purring under the delicate lattice of ribs. The sweetness of the innocent creature kindled the flames in her belly. "I have to get my son."

"It's almost three a.m. You can't go now. We'll go back to the ranch, sleep, talk to Aunt Ginny and Gus and be sure they understand the risks of having you and Ben there."

"No, Mitch. I'm sorry. I have to get him right now. If you don't want to take me, I understand. I have to send Nana Jo home." She struggled to swallow down a lump in her throat. "It's just too dangerous to ask her to stay after what's happened. I need to go it alone now."

"Not alone."

She didn't know what to say to that. It had been a very long time since anyone had stood by her side except for Nana Jo. Certainly not a man. It made her nerves pulse with uncertainty. But it was a mission for Mitch, a means to both assuage his guilt and quench the burning desire for justice. How difficult it must be for him, she thought.

A lawman who had witnessed the worst injustices life could dish out. The kitten mewed, and she wished she had some milk for it.

Finally, he shrugged in resignation. "All right. We'll get Ben and go back to the ranch."

"I can't allow that until Ginny and Gus understand the risk. They don't know about Ben. I can't ask them to become unwilling targets."

He huffed out a breath through his nostrils. "Okay. I'll get a hotel room somewhere. You can sleep there tonight." He shifted. "I'll keep watch in the truck."

She reached a hand and grasped his forearm. "Mitch, I want to be clear about something. I don't blame you for anything that happened to me, so don't blame yourself, either. Don't risk your safety or your family's out of a sense of guilt."

He looked as though he would answer, his eyes drifting over her face as if he was searching for something—a way he'd lost, a truth he'd forgotten. Then he closed his mouth into a thin hard line, put the truck into gear and began to drive.

"The paper," he said after a moment.

"What?"

"The paper in your pocket. What was it?"

She gasped. "I almost forgot. Reporters have been calling the police station to get information on me, one in particular named Elaine Barber. Danny didn't tell her anything." She swallowed. "But there was another call. She identified herself only as number four."

She knew he was scanning his mental catalog of information about Wade's case. He jerked her a look. "Number four? The woman who survived?"

"Bette Whipple."

"She called you?"

"She called Danny, and he took her number."

"Does Foley know?"

"I'm not sure what Danny told him."

"Why does she want to talk to you?"

Jane shook her head. "She's probably terrified to hear that Wade's out. I don't know how she discovered I was in Driftwood. I have to call her."

Mitch's mouth quirked as he considered. "Don't call her until I'm with you."

"She is a victim, too. I have to warn her."

"Tomorrow, when we're clearer, when I've had a chance to think it through."

Jane sighed. "I'm too tired to argue."

"Tell me where we're going and then you can sleep."

"I don't sleep much, not anymore." She directed him out of town and gazed out the window. "I used to sleep like a rock until one night I awakened to find Wade sitting on the edge of the bed, staring at me. I asked him why. He said he wanted to memorize my face while it was young and perfect." She swallowed.

Don't worry, Janey. I'll always try to remember you this way. A bright smile. *Pretty enough to paint.*

Something had bloomed inside her that night, a creeping fear that Wade was not what he seemed to be. Her voice died away, and she shivered. "I never slept soundly after that. I started to snoop then." She blushed. "I looked through some drawers, some files, but I couldn't find anything incriminating except for a bundle of cash and a six-pack of duct tape. I asked him about it and he became furious, said if I ever rifled through his things again I would pay dearly. That's when all the doubts crystallized, all the nagging things I'd ignored. Oh, how

I wish I listened to my instincts sooner." Even now the cold prickled her skin at the memory, her husband's face transformed, as if a mask had been ripped off. "That's when I started making plans to get away." She looked at Mitch. "When did you first know? What Wade really was, I mean?"

Something like pain tightened his mouth, and she thought he would not answer.

"When I was seven, I stopped him from drowning a cat that had scratched him. I knew then."

Without a word, she reached out. His hand was tough and calloused, strong, equally at ease holding a rope or a rifle, yet tender enough to save an orphaned kitten. She put her cheek to the long fingers and they stayed like that for a while, the connection sustaining her as she hoped it did for him.

After a few moments, he cleared his throat and gently pulled his hand away. "Rest now."

The idea of rest was as enticing as an exquisite meal. Her heart was galloping ahead, craving to see her little boy, but fatigue burdened her body with lead weight. She looked at Mitch's profile—stern, hard, steady and honorable, she thought. He might not know it, but he was a good man, she was certain.

Her conscience taunted her. *But didn't you think the same thing of Wade?* Doubt crept in. Wade's shadow stood as it always did, between her and any kind of trusting relationship. What was her heart playing at, urging her to trust her ex-husband's brother? A man who had until recently thought her partner to a serial killer?

But Mitch and Jane had a common bond that no other

people in the world could share—they'd both been close kin to the worst kind of evil, and survived.

Would they be able to do so again?

She wasn't certain, but as she drifted off to sleep, she knew her only chance for herself and Ben was to trust Mitch Whitehorse. She resolved to draw a boundary around her heart. Trust…she told herself…was enough.

It was nearing 3:30 a.m. when Mitch pulled up at the trailer park where Jane had secured a place for Ben and his caretaker. He'd taken extreme care that they not be followed, but the roads were quiet. Here the trailers were set wide apart, with long swatches of grass between them. The unit they were headed for was dark, only the porch lights shining. The entire park was quiet, in fact, except for a dog that barked a few times as the truck rolled by. Jane awakened as Mitch slowed, and she phoned the woman called Nana Jo.

He'd gone to open the passenger door for her, but she was already out and hurrying up the gravel walkway. The trailer door was flung open, and Jane threw herself into the arms of a stocky, gray-haired woman wrapped in a fuzzy robe. He stayed back a piece, since it seemed as though there were tears and tender talk between the two. He took the time to peruse the grounds, but again, there was no sign of movement in the other trailers. Jane gestured for him to join them, and all three stepped inside the trailer. He closed and locked the door.

Nana Jo greeted him with a handshake while Jane immediately disappeared through the doorway into the tiny bedroom.

Nana Jo fixed him with a grave look. "He's still at large?"

"Yes, ma'am."

"Are you going to catch him?"

"Yes, ma'am."

Her eyes narrowed. "The police have hung her out to dry," she said. "As soon as they got their man, they didn't lift a finger to protect her. She's had to live like a stray animal, a fugitive."

And two days ago he'd believed she'd deserved it. He shifted. "I'm not a cop anymore, but I'm going to bring him down."

"He's your brother."

He wondered how much Jane had told her. He stayed silent.

"And she should trust you instead of the cops?" Nana Jo's frown deepened. "Why?"

Why? "Because he'll kill her and take Ben if she doesn't."

Nana Jo watched him for several ticks of the wall clock. She was deciding, taking his measure, as his father would have said, letting her instincts have their way with that uncanny intuition women seemed to possess sometimes. He could see why Jane trusted Ben with Nana Jo.

Another few ticks of the clock, and she gave one small nod. "All right." She went to the table squashed next to the lumpy sofa and pulled a paper from the drawer. "Then I'll give you this."

She handed him a paper with a phone number written on it.

"Whose?"

"Elaine Barber. She's a reporter."

Mitch's stomach dropped. "She called here?"

"Worse." Her mouth pinched. "She showed up this afternoon."

FIFTEEN

Mitch stared. "What did she want?"

"She said she was looking for Jane Reyes. She'd heard from the locals that someone matching her description rented a trailer in town."

Not a big leap. It wasn't tourist season, and news of a newcomer in town wouldn't be much of a secret.

"Of course I told her nothing and sent her away." She bit her lip. "But…"

He braced for it.

"Ben knocked over his blocks and squealed just then, and I think Barber heard."

"So she knows there's a child here."

"Maybe, but she doesn't know it's Jane's."

Mitch wished he felt as certain. "We need to leave."

"Without me."

She said it like a punishment, but while he searched for a response, she held up a palm. "I understand. It will be easier for her to disappear if she needs to, easier for you to hide her if she stands her ground." Nana Jo sighed. "I'll miss that little boy, but I will pray steadfastly that someday she and Ben will be able to stop hiding." There wasn't defeat in the older woman's eyes, but a ferocious gleam similar to what he'd perceived in Jane. The power of prayer—he could not believe in it, but her passion made him regret that he didn't.

She left him to go to the bedroom, returning a moment later. "Well, I just can't. A couple hours won't hurt, will it?"

When he raised a puzzled eyebrow, he followed her to the bedroom. The moonlight poking through the broken blinds painted Jane's face as she lay on her side on the bed, her arms around a little boy curled against her stomach. One chubby hand was out-flung. Nestled above them in the hollow of a pillow was the sleeping kitten. The boy was round cheeked and smaller than Mitch had expected, and his mother… That was what twisted something around in Mitch's insides. Her hair was loose and tangled, skin luminous, mouth curved in an almost smile of pure contentment. He could not identify the feeling that trickled through his senses when he took in mother and child, but it was the same sensation he got early in the morning as he absorbed the view from the saddle, the wide, sweeping green of the ranch land sloping down until it lost itself in the frenetic majesty of the Pacific. Perfect.

That love, that connection, that bond that was born from some sort of goodness he could not fathom. He didn't understand it, or his own reaction, so he reversed from the room.

Nana Jo didn't press. "I'm going to sleep in the other bedroom. Will you be okay on the couch?"

"Yes, ma'am," he said. She padded away. After one more check out the window, he sat in the armchair, since he was a couple of feet too tall to sleep on the couch, and he did not want to shut his eyes, anyway.

Elaine Barber was getting close.

Wade was circling.

Foley was working his own agenda. His jaw clenched.

None of them would get close enough to hurt Jane and her son.

It was his promise to the fragile little family that slept in the next room, a promise he would keep.

"Hi, Mommy. Potty."

The words jolted Jane awake. She sat up, nameless fear quickening her breath until she remembered where she was. Joy took the place of the dread as she smiled at her tousle-haired boy and trailed a fingertip down his cheek, flushed from sleep. Her Ben, her son.

"Nana Jo told me you've been using the potty. Great job, Ben Bear. I'm so proud of you." He put his pointer fingers up and she laughed. He never could repeat her thumbs-up gesture without using the wrong fingers. Such a cheerful child, with no sign of her ex-husband's cruelty, she continually reminded herself. The kitten stretched and kneaded the pillow with tiny paws. Ben's eyes widened at the sight.

"Cat," he squealed.

"Yes, and you can see him after you go potty and have breakfast," Jane insisted. She was surprised that it was almost six and Mitch hadn't woken her. When Ben was finished, she settled him on her hip and went to find Mitch and Nana Jo, drinking coffee in the kitchen. The kitten padded on silent feet after them.

Mitch stood.

Perhaps his size made Ben go shy, because he put his head on Jane's chest, peeking at Mitch with one eye.

"Ben, this is…" Her face went hot. How should she introduce Mitch? "Uh, this is…"

"Mitch," he said, extending a massive palm. Ben surprised her by putting his minuscule hand in Mitch's. "Nice to meet you, Ben."

"You can call him Uncle Mitch," she corrected, letting him down on the floor. Ben was too young to think about the familial connection, she'd decided, and by the time he was old enough to mull it over, they'd be elsewhere, far away from Driftwood, hopefully restarting their lives. It was too bad it couldn't be here, she thought with a pang, in this town of gorgeous views and wide-open spaces.

Ben craned his neck to look up at Mitch and pointed at the kitten nosing around the linoleum. "Cat, Moo Moo."

"Uh, it's Uncle Mitch, not Moo Moo," Jane said, with a laugh. "Sorry, we're still working on our words."

Mitch shrugged, and she thought she caught the glimmer of a smile tugging at the corner of his mouth. "I've been called worse." He took a knee so as to be eye level with Ben.

"Do you like cats, Ben?"

He nodded vigorously.

"What are you going to name him?"

Ben squinched his brows in thought. "Catty Cat."

Mitch did smile now, and she thought the act transformed him into someone altogether different. He laughed, a low, rumbling sound, the first time she'd heard it. Her heart squeezed. Perhaps if Wade had not been Mitch's brother, the stoic mask he wore would not have become permanent.

Nana Jo got Ben settled in a wooden chair with a

toaster waffle. She set the kitten to work lapping at a bowl of milk while Ben watched in absolute fascination.

Mitch sidled closer to Jane and handed her a mug of coffee. "Milk and sugar?"

"Black."

He nodded appreciatively. "We have to go. I've called the ranch already. Ginny and Gus are on board with you and Ben staying there."

"But do they understand…?"

"They understand the risks completely. And what's more, Aunt Ginny said if I don't bring you, she's sending Liam and Chad to fetch us."

Gratitude made her eyes well up. "We'll try not to be a bother."

"No bother, but I want to leave here before sunup."

She lowered her mug, sloshing some on her jeans. "What happened?"

"That reporter came yesterday. She knows there's a child here. Might put things together."

Now Jane was heading for the hallway. "I'll grab Ben's bag."

"I already packed it before you got up," Nana Jo said, patting a duffel bag with a train emblazoned on the front. "Clothes, snacks, shoes and his train collection. Mitch and I got the car seat in the truck already."

Jane saw that Nana Jo already knew of their plans to leave her. "How can I ever thank you?" She hugged Nana tight.

"You come see me when you have your life back," Nana said, through tears. "I will pray for the day I see you and Ben on my doorstep, free of all this."

"Me, too," Jane said, trying to stem her own flow of tears.

She'd just about summoned up the strength to go when there was a knock at the door.

She froze.

"All of you into the bedroom," Mitch growled.

She took Ben by the hand and hurried away, heart thumping.

As Mitch approached the door, he drew a handgun she hadn't known he'd been carrying.

Jane began to pray.

Mitch eyed the stranger out the window, standing in the weak puddle of porch light, a tall woman with glasses, around Mitch's age, probably, wearing jeans and a button-up plaid shirt, her hair pulled into a pony-tail with streaks of gray twined into the dark. She didn't look completely comfortable in the outfit, as if it was a costume she'd put on.

"Be right there," Mitch called. Then he crept out the back door and circled around the front, pulling his re-volver and edging close. The woman whipped around as Mitch came near, surprisingly alert.

She raised her hands, her bulky camera tucked under her shoulder. "Not very neighborly." Her voice was husky, as if she was a smoker.

"Neighbors don't show up before sunrise. What do you want?"

She tried a smile and didn't get one in return, so she shrugged. "I'm Elaine Barber. I'm a reporter."

"For what paper?"

"The *West Coast Bee*."

"Okay. I have nothing to say to a reporter. Get lost."

"I know you're Mitch Whitehorse and I know your family history. Why are you here?"

"I said get lost. You're trespassing."

"But not on your property. This trailer was rented by a woman a week ago. What brings you here?"

"Invited guest. You're not. Time to go."

"Okay." She shrugged. "If you don't want to tell me anything, let me share some conjecture. I think you've got Jane Reyes Whitehorse hidden away in this trailer. Am I right?"

Mitch stepped closer. "You're about to get escorted off this porch step."

Barber backed up a step, palms raised. "Look. This story is hot, and it's going to press one way or another. The climate around here is… Well, let's just say there are locals I've talked to who followed the case closely, and they haven't forgotten all that hate and anger they've stockpiled toward Wade…and his wife."

Anger flashed like an electric shock across his nerves. "Yeah, I guess that's your job, isn't it? To rake up muck to sell a story."

"The muck's already on the surface, once Wade hit town. He burned down your cabin, didn't he?"

Mitch didn't answer.

"If you want to protect Jane Reyes, the best way is to tell me the facts, and we can work out what's safe to reveal."

"I've never met a reporter who cared what kind of damage their stories did."

"I'm not your average reporter," she said.

"It's time for you to go."

"All right, I'll go, but I'll be around." Gingerly, she removed a business card from her pocket and extended it to Mitch, her cell number scrawled on the back.

Mitch didn't take it, so Barber tucked it under the porch mat. "Call me," she said. "Soon."

Mitch waited until Barber's battered Chevy had clattered out of the trailer park before he holstered his weapon and returned to the house.

Jane stood in the kitchen. "I heard what she said. It's all starting again, isn't it?" A glimmer of a bitter smile. "The town will be preparing the tar and feathers."

"No. I won't let that happen."

"Not so long ago you would have been heating that tar along with them."

"I was wrong. So are they."

"What should we do?"

"Load up in the truck."

The seconds that passed between them told him it was another decision point for Jane—whether to continue to trust him or not. He knew from his work with the horses that trust was not a onetime decision. In the beginning it was a series of back-and-forth steps, a constant testing to see how much tension the rope would hold. She had good reasons not to trust him or any man ever again, but he found himself waiting, hoping with every cell that she would believe in him.

After one more endless moment, she turned to the bedroom. "Come on out, Ben Bear. Let's go to Uncle Mitch's ranch."

Mitch blew out a silent breath and ushered them outside. He'd have to be sure the persistent Barber wasn't going to follow them.

Ben hummed a constant stream of songs that Mitch hadn't heard of as they drove back to the ranch, the kitten sitting as close to Ben as it could manage. Mitch didn't think Ben's head was high enough to see out the window until he squealed when they drove onto ranch property.

"Cows!"

Jane laughed. "Yes, Ben. Uncle Mitch works on a cattle ranch."

Mitch waved to Liam, who was returning from his rounds. He was sweaty and dirty and looked profoundly satisfied. He knew the feeling. There was nothing like riding across the sprawling property, keeping tabs on the grass-fed, free-range cattle. The bulls had been turned out with the cows, and the summer months would tell which of the cows were pregnant. In the fall, a whole new group of boisterous calves would be given radio frequency identification tags. The RFID and color-coded tags made it easier to identify the animals from a distance.

Pride swelled inside him. The irrigated pastureland produced adult cattle that tipped the scales at twelve hundred pounds by the time they were two years old. Part of his job was to keep the cattle accustomed to a simple human presence. Without human contact, the animals would quickly become wild.

Liam edged Streak close to the stopped truck, and Mitch heard Ben's inhalation. "Horse," he whispered.

Mitch lowered the rear passenger window. "That's Ben in the back."

Liam thumbed back his cowboy hat, peered into the back seat and waved a leather-gloved hand while Streak lipped the glass. Ben's high-pitched giggle made them all laugh.

"Kid likes horses," Liam said. "Gonna be a regular cowboy someday."

"Yeah," Mitch said, as Liam waved goodbye and

led his horse to the stables. *Of course he's gonna like horses*, Mitch wanted to say. *He's my nephew.* The thought dumbfounded him, along with the prideful sensation in which it was wrapped. He could not possibly feel as though Ben, a boy he'd just met, from a brother he could not stand to think about, was his kin. He was so unsettled at his own reaction, he bypassed the house, mechanically heading for the stables. Reversing course, he took them back.

Helen's van was parked there, Roughwater Lodge emblazoned on the side. He held the car door while Jane extracted Ben from the complicated car seat straps. She wanted to carry him, but the boy insisted on walking, clutching her hand. Gutsy, Mitch thought, in admiration. He had Jane's narrow face, but he thought he could detect the long-legged stature of the Whitehorse clan. That almost made him stop. This was Wade's son. Had Wade's twisted sickness been passed down in the DNA? He figured Jane must have spent a lot of time worrying about that very thing.

But Wade and Mitch were both the product of the same parents, and they couldn't be more different. He considered the passion burning inside him to capture Wade. Both brothers were ferociously determined. *Two sides of the same coin?* He swallowed hard and ushered them into the house.

SIXTEEN

A woman greeted them in the foyer, her long auburn hair tied back in a ponytail. A pencil poked out from just above the hair tie, where she must have tucked it. She immediately held out a hand to Jane. "Helen Pike," she said. "I'm Liam's sister."

Jane noted the wide smile that mirrored her brother's, the eyes a similar shade of blue, striking against her freckled skin. She introduced herself, and Helen bent to wiggle her fingers at Ben. "Hi, sweetie. I brought some toys for you to play with."

"Oh, that was so kind, but you didn't need to do that," Jane protested.

"I manage the Roughwater Lodge about two miles from here. We have a whole kids' area and more toys than we can store. Besides, I love playing blocks, and I don't have a building pal."

"I didn't know there was a lodge on the property."

"Ranching is always capital intensive and return deficient."

Jane found herself grinning at this outgoing woman who spoke about business and blocks in the same breath.

Mitch chuckled. "You can tell she has way too many college degrees. She's as smart as her brother."

"Smarter," Helen said with a wink. "What a sweet little kitty," she said as Ben pointed to the kitten wiggling in the crook of Jane's arm.

"Catty Cat," Ben said solemnly.

"Of course. What else would you call a cat?" Helen said with a laugh. As her gaze traveled to Ben, Jane thought she saw a haze of sadness momentarily dull Helen's good cheer. "He reminds me of...a friend of mine. She had twin girls. They must be about this age by now. I haven't seen them since they were a few months old."

Jane nodded. "Time goes by so fast sometimes. It's hard to stay in touch."

"Their mother was my best friend. She, um, died a year ago." A ten-second pause before she whispered the rest, so low Jane almost missed it. "She was murdered, actually."

"I'm so sorry," Jane said.

"Me, too." Helen blew out a breath and shook her head before the smile was back in place. "Anyway, the toys are in the dining room. Want to see them, Ben?"

Ben nodded, and they trekked into the living room, where Ginny joined them, an iPad tucked under her arm. She gasped in delight when she saw Ben.

"Well, hello, Ben. I'm Aunt Ginny. I'm so happy you're here to visit."

Ben didn't say anything, but his eyes rounded at the sight of a basket filled with toy cars. He beelined right for them, hunkering down on the throw rug, Catty Cat pawing curiously at the pile.

Jane sat next to him, exclaiming over each one as

Ben showed it to her. Helen caught Mitch's eye. Wordlessly he followed her to the far side of the room. Jane didn't want to eavesdrop, but she found herself wondering what they were discussing as Mitch's face went dark with anger. Finally, he gestured her over. "You have a right to hear this. Tell her, Helen."

Helen fingered the zipper of her jacket. "I was in town this morning at the Chuckwagon. It's the town's primary eatery in Driftwood. I overheard some...talk."

She waited, tension gathering in her stomach.

Helen looked pained. "Just some locals—not everyone, of course. A few loudmouths, is all."

"Just say it, Helen," Mitch said.

She straightened, keeping her voice low. Liam approached on socked feet and planted a kiss on her cheek.

"What did I interrupt?"

"I was mentioning that there's talk in town, the Judd boys in particular."

"Hotheads," Liam said.

"Not unlike you, from time to time," Helen reprimanded, "but they'd heard about the fire, and they'd also heard it was likely Wade's work."

Mitch sighed. "It was a matter of time before that got out, especially with a reporter sniffing around."

"They'd also heard..." She shot a hasty look at Jane. "That Jane was hiding out somewhere in the area. They think... I mean...they said..."

"That they hated me?" Jane did not need confirmation to know her guess was accurate.

"I'm sorry," Helen said. "I just thought it would be better for you not to be surprised."

"It's not a surprise," Jane said, fighting back the despair. "People will never stop thinking I helped Wade.

They've always found out somehow about my past even after I dropped the Whitehorse name, and that's when the hate mail, the smashed windows, the graffiti always starts up." She shook her head. "I shouldn't stay here. If they find out…"

"They won't, and if they do, I'd deal with it," Mitch said.

Liam lifted an eyebrow. "And you'd have help."

Twin pangs of regret and gratitude throbbed in Jane's heart. "I can't allow anyone to be hurt because they offered me shelter."

"We'll be careful."

Until Wade was captured, it was dangerous for them all if she stayed and dangerous for her and Ben to leave. Caught in an impossible situation, like she had been ever since she married Wade. Unable to speak over the lump in her throat, she answered with a nod and then wandered away to watch her son play.

The day passed in a blur. By early evening, Ben was tired, so she laid him on the guest room bed. Catty Cat, now freshly washed and fed thanks to Helen, had been set up with a litter box. He leaped up and snuggled at the top of Ben's pillow, just like he'd done in the trailer. Ben's eyes were half-closed by the time she kissed him, stroked Catty Cat and tiptoed out of the room.

Desperate to clear her mind, she let herself out into a golden sunset, zipping her jacket against the chill. Breathing in the mingled scents of grassland and sea, she spotted Mitch leaning against the fence, staring out toward the ocean as the sun sank in glowing splendor into the waves. He wore jeans and a cowboy hat, leather gloves tucked into his back pocket. His boots were worn and scuffed, tough, like the cowboy who wore them. There was no pretense about Mitch White-horse; he wore no mask of self-importance. He was an honest, hardworking ranch hand, and his straight-forwardness pulled her like the tide. She went to him, following his line of sight past the smooth hollows of green, backed by rocky hillsides, out to the restless sea.

"It's beautiful here," she said, coming to stand next to him.

"Yeah."

"I'm…I'm not sure it's right to stay."

He didn't look at her, the wind tangling her long hair with his. "To whip up or whoa," he said.

"What?"

"Decisions have to be made. When the cattle are moving in the wrong direction, you gotta whip up, ride hard and get ahead of them or send the dogs to turn them. When they're moving in the right direction, you back off and give them space to do the right thing."

She smiled. "If only people were as easy to man-age as cattle."

He grimaced. "I didn't mean to compare the two."

"Yes, you did, but it's okay. I take no offense. I've been mulling it over again and again, and it's come down to three choices. Trust Foley, trust you or trust neither of you and go it alone. I've prayed about it, and for some reason I think God's telling me to trust you."

She saw his jaw tighten, shadowed by the hint of a dark beard.

"I won't let you down."

She touched his arm, rock solid, steel taut. "I know that in my head. It's just…hard to convince my heart."

Their gaze wandered to the lush grassland now darkening in dusk. "So I guess that means I'll whoa for a while."

He smiled. "Sounds funny when you say it."

"A hopeless city slicker."

"Yeah." A smile still played on his lips. "But I can teach Ben a few things so he won't be such a townie, as Liam would say."

"He'd love that." She tucked her hair behind her ear. "Why did you choose the cowboy life after you retired from the marshals?"

"Suits me."

"How so?"

"I'm a good tracker, horseman. I'm patient, and I'm happy to work by myself. I've got an eye for noticing things in the cattle—illnesses, behavioral changes."

"That's the only reason? You have suitable cowboy skills?" With anyone else she would never have engaged in such a personal conversation, but with Mitch, it felt different. It felt…safe.

She gave him time to find the answer.

"Here it's…the way things should be. There's dignity and respect for people and animals. Ranchers don't threaten to use lawyers in place of an honest conversation and handshake. There's honor in that."

"And there's honor in you," she said before she stopped herself.

He went quiet, studying his boots. Her cheeks burned as she stood shoulder to shoulder with him, this ally, this stalwart rock of a man whom her prayers told her she could trust. Being near him made her question herself, her ideas, her feelings. It was dangerous, she thought, yet she did not want to walk away, not yet.

"I haven't been a good man, or a kind man, but I'm

gonna try and be better." He ignored a moth that flitted past. "So I can help you and Ben."

In the distance the stars began to glimmer as the sea-scented fog rolled in low along the coast. She tipped her face upward. "You know, I haven't looked up at the stars in ages. I guess when you're running, you're always looking just ahead." The spangle of constellations still visible above the fog took her breath away. "Magnificent."

He nodded, and she realized he was looking at her. The dusk stripped away the hardness from his features and gentled him, this giant of a man. Again she felt the reckless desire to share what was on her heart. "I don't know how this will turn out, Mitch, or why God put us together here in the middle of this wild place, but I am grateful that He did."

He turned to her then. His hand moved slowly, wonderingly as he traced the contours of her face with his calloused fingers. "I…" He looked at her a moment longer.

Whip up or whoa? her heart whispered as he moved closer, his mouth so close, his eyes so intense. Should she let her feelings step over the line past ally to something more? Or retreat behind the lonely walls she'd built to protect herself and Ben?

His lips twitched, and he fit his mouth to hers, gently, tenderly, and her heart broke into a million flecks of golden light. In that one connection, she felt what it must be like to trust, to be part of a healthy, pure love, a connection so sweet she did not know where he ended and she began.

Until panic crept in.

Trust and connection…like she thought she'd had with Wade.

Mitch was attracted to her, undoubtedly, like she to him. Why? Was it something in her that drew the men from the Whitehorse family? Did Mitch see in her a pretty face that he wanted to own, to mold, to control, like Wade had? Her brain said no, but her heart pounded in disagreement.

Panic overwhelmed her, and she pulled away so fast she stumbled. He reached and held her steady, and they both struggled to catch their breath.

"Did I…? I mean…" he mumbled.

"It was a mistake, that's all," she panted. "Just forget it."

He blinked at her with those black eyes, so unlike Wade's that she could almost convince herself they weren't brothers. Almost.

"Didn't feel like a mistake to me," he said quietly.

"I'm…I'm going to go check on Ben." Turning on her heel, she ran back into the shelter of the ranch house.

SEVENTEEN

He wanted to apologize the next morning after he'd listened to Aunt Ginny's Sunday Bible class, the one she insisted on teaching for the early-shift cowboys who didn't attend church. At least, an apology was what he figured he should do, but that kiss, the one he'd shared with Jane, felt way more right than wrong. He didn't regret it one bit, but clearly it had felt like a mistake to Jane. And why wouldn't it? The list was long, he thought bitterly.

She'd been married to his monster of a brother.

Her life and her son's were in danger.

She could not trust herself and her own instincts.

He'd shown her the same unjust judgment as everybody else until recently.

All great reasons why he should not have sought that kiss, and definitely why he should not ever seek one from her again. He tried to focus on his research, an hour stolen between checking the fence line and helping Liam repair the irrigation to the southernmost pasture. He'd asked Helen to pick up a rocking chair at the flea market, and he set about painting it, imagining Jane cuddling with Ben, if Mitch ever had the courage to give it to her now. Even with the distractions, his police brain would not shut down. Three things… Wade needed three things to survive: money, shelter, communication. Where was he getting it? Fugitives typically went to family members, but that wasn't going to help in this case. Friends? He didn't think Wade had any. The only girlfriend he'd known about was Tanya, the daughter of the gas station owner, but Mitch could not find her via any of his research. He no longer had access to the vast police databases. He didn't want to contact Foley, but he could not think of any other choices.

Foley listened without interrupting. "What's the girl's name?"

"Tanya Alder."

He huffed. "And you tried to find her, didn't you?" He laughed. "Not so easy now that you're on the civilian side. We'll track her down. Don't worry."

Mitch ground his teeth. He did not want to work with Foley, but there was no getting around it. "I'm sure Danny told you that Bette Whipple left a number for Jane."

"Has she called her?"

"Not yet."

"We found her apartment in SoCal pretty easily, but she's not there. We left a message with her apartment manager for her to call us. Dumb to reach out to Jane."

"She's scared."

"But she's contacting the one person who Wade wants more than anything. That makes her a target, too. Bad judgment."

"Like I said, she's scared. What have you got on Wade?"

"Nothing I'm going to share with you, other than my people are on it."

He hadn't expected anything in return, especially not from Foley, and none of his other former colleagues would answer his calls. Again, not unexpected.

"I know you don't want to, Mitch, but keep me posted."

He hung up and saddled Rosie, hoping the hard physical ranch duty would knock something loose in his brain. When the job was done, he returned to the house.

Jane finally emerged around lunchtime, fixing Ben a plate with a cheese sandwich and a glass of milk, nothing for herself. Her focus was on her son, avoiding any eye contact with Mitch. He finally caught her elbow as she headed to the kitchen to help wash the dishes.

"We need to talk." He saw a flash of panic in her eyes. "About when to call Bette."

She relaxed a fraction. "Oh. Okay. As soon as possible, I think. I'm worried about her."

"When you get Ben settled, use my phone. I'll listen in, with your permission."

She hesitated only for a moment. "Okay."

Okay. She still trusted him in spite of the kiss, at least to a point. It was the best he could ask for.

Aunt Ginny and Helen settled with Ben in front of the TV, watching a movie about some sort of animated train. Ben was enthralled, and Ginny was pink cheeked with happiness at sharing the moment with the little boy. Helen was also partaking in the spoiling, preparing them all glasses of chocolate milk, but he noted the faraway look on her face when she watched Ben and he knew the proximity brought back painful wounds that had not scabbed over.

He and Jane went outside to the sprawling flagstone porch and sat. The area provided an unobstructed view of the cattle dotting the land below. She looked dwarfed and delicate by the surroundings, and he wished fervently in that moment that they could sit there under different circumstances, without the mountain of fear, the menace of his brother, the discomfort he'd caused her with his kiss. Shaking away the thought, he handed her the phone.

After a breath, Jane dialed, pressing the speaker button.

On the second ring, a woman answered, her voice high and reedy.

"Hello?"

"Is this Bette?"

"Jane," the woman said. "I've been searching for you."

Jane felt a rush of joy and anxiety. "I'm so glad to talk to you."

Her words spilled out in a cascade. "After the trial, I got your letter, and I realized then that you didn't know anything about Wade and what he did to me."

Jane gulped. Wade had befriended Bette at a gym, pretended to be interested in her, until he abducted and imprisoned her on their property, intending to force her to withdraw her savings, like he had with the others. She'd escaped, heading to the police and setting his eventual arrest in motion.

"I'm so happy to hear your voice." Bette's crying carried clearly over the line.

Jane bit her lip. "Are you okay? I mean…are you safe right now?"

"Yes, so far, but I heard— I mean, I know he's out. Is he after us?"

She heard the rising hysteria. "Calm down," Jane said soothingly. "He's after me, but there's no reason to think he's found you, too." Mitch gestured for her to ask a question. "How did you know to leave your number at the Driftwood police station?"

"I remembered from the trial that Wade had a brother, a US marshal. I did some research online."

Mitch frowned. Jane knew he'd been careful to keep his name out of things, to live as silently and anonymously as he could. Bette went on to explain.

"There was a cattle auction a couple years back and his name was on a public document—Mitch's, I mean."

One error and she'd caught it. Jane bit back a sigh. A very smart woman, Bette Whipple. Wade had always targeted bright women—their only flaw was trusting too much.

"I'm scared," Bette said. "After the trial I left my nursing job, did some computer work from wherever I was staying. I even started on my dream of getting a master's at a local college, but now he's out and I can't think of anything else." Sobs choked off her words. Jane gripped the phone.

"He won't find you."

"Yes, he will. He will. I keep imagining I see him everywhere I go."

"No," Jane said firmly. "He's here." She caught Mitch's warning look. "He's after me and Mitch. You're safe. Please listen. You're safe."

"I need to see you," she babbled. "Please, Jane. I'm scared. I made a mistake."

"What mistake?"

"Coming here…to Driftwood."

Jane jerked in shock. "Here? Why would you come here?"

"I wanted to find you, to talk to you. Now I'm stuck. I'm running out of money, and I'm scared."

"Where are you?" Jane demanded. "Tell me right now and I'll get the police…"

"No police," Bette almost shouted. "They're in league with Wade—he's paid them off. He had money hidden somewhere. They helped him escape."

"How do you know…?"

"I have to go. I'm in a bad place. I'll call you again."

"No, Bette. Don't hang up," Jane pleaded, but the line went dead.

Jane looked at Mitch in horror. He was already reaching for the phone. "I'll call Danny. He's a good man. He'll have to loop Foley in, but maybe not right away."

Jane's nostrils flared, lips crushed in a tight line. He reached for her hand, the fingers dead cold. "It will be okay. They'll find her."

"What if Wade finds her first?"

He didn't answer.

She fought for calm. "I let Wade victimize those women. It's too late for them, but not for her, not for Bette. I can't let him do it again."

He pulled her to him and hung on while she cried. When she was able to breathe more normally, he settled her on a chair and dialed Danny Patron's number.

EIGHTEEN

Sunday morphed to Monday, and still there was no further word from Bette. Jane was consumed with worry. Danny called twice to tell them he could find no sign of her in town, though the gas station attendant had noticed a woman driving a compact car the day before. He'd remembered the dark-haired passenger with sunglasses because strangers to town, especially young women traveling alone, were a novelty. He had not noticed where she'd gone.

Mitch was busy with his ranch duties, and she could tell by his expression when he returned from the pasture astride Rosie that he had not heard further about Bette.

Thinking of the woman's fear stirred a deep ache in her heart. She'd failed Bette before with her own ignorance, and she desperately wanted to help her now, get her to a safe place far away from Wade.

She tried to distract herself from the madness by helping Aunt Ginny bake up a half-dozen pies. Ben assisted, too, making his own lopsided pie specimens with bits of leftover dough. Catty Cat sat on a cushion in the corner, basking in a sunbeam. Jane was happy to see the kitten looking a bit fuller, with a pronounced pinkness to the little nose.

"Uncle Moo Moo," Ben chortled as Mitch loped into the kitchen.

Liam, who had appointed himself official taste tester, chowing down his second slice of pie, almost choked on a mouthful. Recovering, he laughed until tears ran down his face. "Did I hear that right?"

"I like it," Aunt Ginny said. "Even better than Aunt Ginny."

"Uncle Moo Moo, that is the best thing I've ever heard," Liam said, wiping his eyes. "I am totally blabbing that news all over town."

Jane tensed, and Liam caught her panicked look.

"Okay. Maybe not all over town, at least until after the current situation is resolved, but I'm going to keep it in my back pocket, for sure."

Mitch shot him a look but grabbed a bottle of water from the fridge and slid into a chair next to Ben. "You makin' a pie?"

"A choo twain," Ben said.

Mitch looked to Jane for explanation.

"He's making a choo-choo train."

Mitch's face brightened. "Oh, yeah. I see it now. Say, I've got something for you, if you're done."

Ben nodded, and Jane wiped his hands. They followed Mitch out of the ranch house, leaving Liam still chuckling in the kitchen. They walked down a graveled drive to a neat workshop hidden by a copse of trees.

"Liam does his saddle work here, but he lets me have a corner."

Mitch took a box down from a wooden shelf and extracted an object for Ben.

Ben's eyes went wide, his mouth open as he yelled. "Twain!"

It was a painted wooden train with sturdy red wheels. Mitch handed him two more. "And here's the locomotive and there's the last one. Know what that's called?"

"Boose!"

"Yeah, a caboose." He pointed to the metal disks on the ends of the cars. "These are magnets, so you can hook the cars to the locomotive, just like real trains."

Ben hugged the trains to his chest.

Jane thought she had never seen her son so happy, and it robbed her of breath for a moment. When she recovered, she tapped Ben on the shoulder. "What should we say to Uncle Mitch?"

Ben tore his gaze from the trains, wrestled a hand loose from his toys and hugged Mitch around the knees. "Fank you, Uncle Moo Moo," he said into Mitch's knee-caps.

Mitch shot her a look, half startled, half befuddled. She smiled because she feared her voice might have a hitch.

He sank down to his knees and carefully embraced Ben as if he would break at any moment. "You're welcome," he said.

Then Ben hugged his toys again. "Play?"

"Yes, we should play with them right now," she affirmed. "Let's go back to the house, okay?" They walked together, Ben nearly dancing with delight over his new toys.

"That was so sweet, Mitch. Really."

He shrugged. "Ah. I got into making trains about ten years ago. I had to figure out the proper way to make a toddler version, but I think it turned out okay."

"More than okay." She reached out and squeezed his hand.

Head ducked, he squeezed it back.

On their return trip, they met Uncle Gus guiding a foal by a lead rope. The gawky creature half walked, half hopped along.

"That's Sugar," Mitch said. "She's a handful."

Uncle Gus greeted them and let Ben stroke the velvety nose of the young horse. "Just got her vaccinations," he said. "So now she gets some playtime." Sugar lipped at Ben's hair, which made them all laugh. The gangly creature was as curious about her son as he was of her.

Uncle Gus led the horse away, Ben still staring, trains clutched tight.

"Maybe when she's a little older, you could ride her, Ben. I could show you how." Mitch meant no harm by the offer, but Jane bit her lip and Mitch noticed immediately.

"I...uh, I said the wrong thing, didn't I?" he said as they led Ben back to the house.

"No, not really. It was a lovely thing to tell him, but I don't know where we will be next week, let alone next month. I've never... I mean, I haven't been able to give him a settled life before."

Mitch squared his shoulders. "You will when we put Wade away."

"I want to believe that with everything in my soul, but that day may never come. I can't live here, sponging off Gus and Aunt Ginny indefinitely."

"You're not. They don't see it that way." He paused, and something changed in his tone. "I don't see it that way."

The words warmed her, bloomed feelings that she

had never experienced before, like the first taste of an exotic fruit. It was a heady feeling, dizzying. *But you can't have those kind of thoughts for Mitch, especially not now.* "Well, anyway, it was a kind offer, and your gift to Ben was perfect. He's over the moon." There, she thought she'd put them back on the right track, normal ground, until he turned her to face him.

"I've been thinking about what you said about not living like I have a future. Seems to me that my job right now is to make sure you and Ben have one, and then, well, it also seems to me like you get to choose where to spend it."

She froze as he stroked a finger along her cheek.

"This place would be a great spot for starting over," he murmured.

For one sliver of a second she wanted nothing more than to lean in close to him, to give in to the feelings that crowded and danced like moths circling a flame.

"I can't, Mitch. I can't think of that."

"You can if you let yourself."

"With Wade…with everything… I can't allow my heart to go there. You're his…"

"Brother?" The word came out hard and clipped as he stepped back. "I know. Does that mean I can never be anything else in your mind?"

She sought helplessly for something to say to ease the blow she'd just delivered.

His frown deepened. "You want people to see you apart from your relationship with Wade. How come you can't do that for me?"

There was no answer. The black of his eyes dulled to a flat, hopeless sheen. She thought he might speak again, but instead he walked away, his long strides eating up the ground, restoring the distance between them.

Mitch awakened at 4:00 a.m., his accustomed hour, and rolled out of bed in the bunkhouse to find a message on his phone.

"It's Bette. I'm sorry I hung up on you. I got scared. Meet me in town, okay? Today. Eight o'clock at the Chuckwagon Diner. Don't bring the police. I told you they are on the take. I just want to talk to you. It would help me sort things out. Please." The message ended.

He threw on his clothes and boots and went to wake Liam.

Liam sat up, one eye open and one closed. Mitch launched into the story until Liam held up a finger. "One sec." He put the tiny hearing aid in his left ear. "Okay. Now I'm at least going to get the gist."

He listened, propped up on his palms. "So how do you want to play it?"

"I can't risk Jane's safety. I will go meet Bette, find out what she wants. Help her get someplace safe. You make sure Wade doesn't have eyes on her, watch for any sign of him. Can you call Torey at the Chuckwagon and tell her to save that booth in the back for us?"

"Right," Liam said, throwing off the covers. "I got your back." He said the rest low. "Uncle Moo Moo."

Mitch let himself out of the house and climbed into his truck. A few minutes later, Liam pulled up behind in his vehicle looking sheepish. That was when he noticed Jane storming out of the ranch house, beelining for him. She marched over to Mitch, but before she got there, Liam leaned out the window.

"Sorry, man," Liam said. "I called from the kitchen,

and she heard me talking to Torey requesting a back booth. She put the rest together."

"You were going to meet Bette without me," Jane fired at Mitch.

"Safer."

Liam rolled away, giving him a look that read *Glad it isn't me.*

"Don't you understand?" Jane's lips were trembling. "I have to help her, me. I'm the one that let her get hurt. I have to make that right." The courage stunned him, the grit. A buzz raced around his stomach that he had not felt since his long-ago days with Paige Lynn. *Knock it off. You know where she stands on that, since you went on and made a fool of yourself yesterday.* He swallowed.

"You are not responsible for what happened to Bette. Wade is."

Her eyes flashed lightning at him, and he wished he could capture her intensity in a photo so he would always be able to remember.

"That's rich coming from you. Let's get real here, Mitch," she said. "You feel responsible for Wade's actions. That's why you're helping me, isn't it? Helping me and Ben?"

"Maybe at first."

"Well, why now? I'm just a means to assuage your guilt." Tears sparked in her eyes. "You are using me just like your brother did."

He fought down the swirl of anger. "You know that's not true. You're picking a fight because it's easier that way, simpler."

She stopped then. "Mitch, you're looking to soothe your own guilt and nothing more. I can see that now." She waved a hand. "All this talk of the future here for us in Driftwood. You've convinced yourself you have feelings for me because you want to make up for what Wade did to us. I'm the poor wounded kitten that needs tending after your brother crushed me under his heel. Is that it?"

He waited a beat, the vein in his jaw jumping. "Finished?"

"Not until you tell me what I want to hear. The truth."

"I'll give you the truth, Jane, but it's not gonna be what you want." He couldn't put together the words to tell her that an inexplicable sensation had begun to creep through his body since she'd come to stay at the ranch, past the pain and the granite walls of self-protection and the anger that he'd nursed his whole life long. He didn't understand what was happening well enough to put it into words. Instead he pulled her to his open window and kissed her, holding her close with a palm around the back of her neck, a warm hollow in her nest of silken hair.

He felt her start before she kissed him back, lips warm and satin, vibrant and life giving, and for a brief moment, one spectacular blip in time, he forgot that she was his brother's ex-wife, forgot his solitary mantra and let slip from his mind all other thoughts. He felt love, truth be told, pure and potent, that undercut the rock cliff of hatred in his heart.

The kiss was both endless and too brief. She moved back, breathing unsteadily. "Mitch, this can't happen. I won't let it."

And all at once he was slapped with the reality of what he'd done. Again. He closed his eyes, heard her breath catch.

"I didn't mean to hurt you," she whispered, mouth trembling.

He blushed and got out, heading for the passenger side to open the door for her, silent while she approached.

She put a hand on his bicep, and it immobilized him.

"I mean, if I could ever learn to trust someone again, I'd want a man like you."

A man like you...

"I get it," he rasped. "You said it before in so many words. Message delivered."

Her head dropped.

"But just so you know, Jane, my feelings don't come from guilt. It's a shame that yours do."

"Mitch," she whispered, and there was heartbreak in the way she said it. "I'm sorry."

He waited for her to get in, shut the door and drowned out those two words in the gunning of the engine. Wade had run off Paige Lynn, and now, Mitch finally understood, Wade's shadow would forever stand firmly between him and Jane. He didn't allow himself to think about what could have been, in another time, another place.

Whip up or whoa.

It was definitely time to whoa.

He would give her a future, her and Ben, and then he would watch her ride out of his life.

Another win for Wade.

If God was the God of love, he wondered, why did evil win the day again?

Without another word, he took the road toward town.

NINETEEN

Jane sat in misery, relieved when Mitch pulled to the curb on a Driftwood side street. She wanted to say something, anything, to erase the hurt she'd caused him, caused them both. She wanted to love not just a man *like* Mitch, but Mitch himself, but how could she possibly give her heart to Wade's brother? Even if she was willing to risk stepping out on the tightrope of trust again, she could not and would not consider a relationship that would confuse Ben when he was old enough to process it all.

I fell in love with your uncle. It would be impossible to explain, even if Mitch's feelings for her did light her soul in ways she'd never felt before. And why was she spending any emotional energy on the future when Wade was still free to terrorize?

She got out of the truck before Mitch could approach to open her door, sucking in lungfuls of crisp air that brought her back to the present moment. Bette. She had to find Bette and help her by convincing her to get out of Driftwood immediately.

Mitch joined her on the sidewalk. Their location was quiet, along a tree-lined street sprinkled with old ranch-style homes with plenty of green yards between them. At the end of the block, where the street joined the main drag, she noticed the white awnings that indicated some sort of event, barricades preventing traffic from entering.

Mitch stared, frowning. Liam drove up and rolled down his window.

"What's going on?"

"Tuesday Stroll."

"What's that?"

"Man, you don't get out much, do you? It's a farmers' market, every Tuesday, year-round."

Mitch glowered. "Great."

"Give me five. I'll double back and get a seat in the Chuckwagon."

"Stay under the radar in case I need you."

Liam grinned wolfishly. "I'm way too good-lookin' to stay out of the spotlight, but I reckon I can give it a try."

He winked at Jane, who could not resist a giggle, turned the truck and rumbled away.

Jane started toward the corner, and Mitch caught up in one long stride. He reached for her arm, but she kept going.

"This doesn't feel right," he started.

"I'll talk to her, convince her to go. We're in a public place, and Wade's gone silent. It's possible he's moved on anyway." She forced a confident tone that she did not feel.

Mitch walked next to her, tense as a wildcat, shoulders stiff. She reached the corner, stepped out into the main street, which was lined with booths piled high with apples, winter squash, homemade pecan pies and olive oils. One merchant offered freshly caught fish, glistening on beds of ice. Dozens of people meandered along, chatting and filling canvas bags with their choices. Jane scanned the group as they walked for any sign of Bette. The last time she'd seen her at the trial, Bette had been a whip-thin, angular woman, tall, with blond hair and thin lips.

Through a break in the booths, she saw the Chuck-wagon Diner. Two large wooden wagon wheels stood sentry at either side of the neatly painted building, the beige walls accented by maroon trim around the windows. Patrons sat at tables sipping sodas and enjoying plates overflowing with eggs, bacon and fluffy white biscuits.

Mitch put a hand on her lower back to steer her toward the building when a woman stepped from behind a display of jellies and jams. She was tall, fuller cheeked than Jane remembered, and her hair was dark now, her eyes magnified by chic glasses.

Jane's breath caught, and suddenly she was back at the trial, mourning what her ignorance had cost an innocent young woman. Fragments of memory stabbed through her mind.

I thought he was a nice guy.

He was friendly, took an interest in me.

I didn't see him clearly until it was too late.

Jane could have uttered the exact same sentiments herself, along with a few more.

But you were his wife—you, more than anyone else, should have known.

She pulled in a steadying breath and wrapped Bette in a hug. The two women clung to each other.

Bette Whipple looked like a college student. She wore a yellow T-shirt emblazoned with a blue bird. The Fighting Falcons football team. The symbol seemed to represent the life Bette should have had, if Wade hadn't interrupted.

"I'm so glad to see you," Jane managed.

"Me, too," Bette murmured in her ear.

She could feel Bette trembling, the tiny shivers that racked her body.

"Let's get you both inside," Mitch said.

As Jane was drawing away, she heard Bette gasp. Bette's eyes rounded, and her mouth tightened into a shocked circle.

"What? What is it?" Jane said, trying to reach for her hand.

"I saw him," Bette said. "Across the street. He just went into the hardware store."

Mitch was taking out his phone. "Inside the restaurant. Now." Then he bolted across the street.

Bette gripped Jane's arm. "We have to run. We have to get away."

Together they raced toward the restaurant, but instead of entering, Bette sprinted past.

"No, we have to go inside," Jane called, reaching to catch her arm and turn her. "Bette, stop."

Bette was running blindly, staggering against a market booth and toppling some jars of jelly. In the confusion, several shoppers scurried to retrieve the fallen jars.

"Stop," Jane called as she trailed Bette down an alley between the restaurant building and the small post office next to it. "We have to go back to the restaurant."

Still Bette continued on, plunging deeper into the alley, her out-flung fingers grazing over the rough bricks as she ran. Jane understood the desire to run from Wade, to flee as far and as fast as possible without allowing reason to enter into the picture. She should double back, find Mitch or Liam, stay safe, but how could she abandon Bette to Wade again?

Before her mind could consider the consequences, she sprinted after her.

"Bette," she yelled as she ran. "Please stop."

The alley opened onto a back lot for overflow parking. A few dozen cars filled in some of the spaces. Against the wall was a dumpster and a cart stacked with flattened boxes. The rear side of the lot edged a cluster of trees, and she could hear the gurgle of a river over the wild beating of her own heart.

"Bette, where are you?" Her voice was urgent, edged with fear she could not control. She did not think Wade would have had time enough to spot them and evade Mitch, but she didn't put anything past him. If he was anywhere in the vicinity, they were both in grave danger.

A dark head popped up from behind a car. Jane blew out a breath and went to her. Bette was crying.

Jane embraced her, patting her back like she did with Ben when he had a nightmare. "I'm sorry," Bette sobbed.

"It's okay. You got scared. I understand. It's okay now. Let's go back in the restaurant. We'll be safe there."

Bette wiped her tearstained face. She looked around, dazed, Jane thought. "Where…?"

"We're behind the Chuckwagon. It's okay. We'll just double back and stay with Liam until Mitch says it's clear."

Bette didn't answer. Jane put her hands around Bette's face, cupping her cheeks. "Look at me."

Bette dragged her eyes to meet Jane's, the pale green

of her irises picking up the morning sunlight. "Take three deep breaths, okay? I'll do it with you."

They breathed together until Bette gave her a smile, stronger than she'd expected. Bette was a fighter, deep down, Jane thought.

"Can you walk back with me now?"

Bette nodded, looking around the perimeter of the lot as if she expected Wade to appear at any moment. Wind picked up a torn piece of cardboard and sent it skittering along, making Jane jump. The hum of the restaurant kitchen noises filtered through the air, comforting Jane. They were so close to people, to help.

"Let's go," she said to Bette.

Bette nodded and crept out from her hiding spot.

Jane ushered her forward just as a car roared up. From behind the wheel, Wade smiled as he jerked the car into Park and leaped from the driver's seat.

After a second of sheer, immobilizing panic, adrenaline flooded her body. "Run," she screamed to Bette, shoving her forward. Bette took off, legs churning. Jane darted behind her, terror balling up her muscles. She'd made it only a couple of car lengths when Wade caught her, bringing her to the ground.

TWENTY

Mitch had searched all the aisles in the hardware store and found no sign of his brother. He pushed out the back exit, taking in the empty lot in seconds. No Wade.

He was about to return to the store when the door was pushed slowly open. Mitch flattened himself against the wall and waited. This time he had the advantage. An arm came through, and all of a sudden the door slammed open. Mitch grabbed the arm and swung the newcomer off balance. The figure lurched forward onto her face at the same moment Mitch realized it was not his brother.

"What are you doing here?" he barked at Elaine Barber.

Barber raised her palms a few inches off the asphalt in a gesture of surrender. "I saw you charge in. I figured you were after Wade."

"So you decided to get a story for yourself." Mitch shook his head in disgust, grabbing her palm and hoisting her to her feet. "I could have shot you."

"Then I guess I'd have grounds for a lawsuit and a good story."

Mitch didn't honor that with a reply. He left the reporter there and pushed back into the store and found the owner behind the counter.

"Herb, did you see anyone duck in here?"

Herb raised an eyebrow. "Looking for your brother, Mitch?"

Mitch felt the bile burning his throat and nodded.

Herb poured nails out of a bag onto the counter and began to sort them. "I've heard plenty of rumors. Heard you might even be helping out Wade's wife."

"She's his ex-wife, and she didn't know anything about what he did."

"Yeah?" Herb continued to sort the nails, piling the largest into the jar. "She'd have to be pretty clueless, wouldn't she?"

He bit back the angry thoughts. "So did you see Wade or not?"

"No, but if he's in town, you'd better keep an eye out, especially if you're cuddling up to his wife."

Mitch slammed out the front door. He scanned the street and found no sign of Wade. He was threading through the market shoppers to get to the restaurant when Liam called.

"They never made it in. On my way out back right now."

The trickle of fear in his belly morphed into a raging torrent. "I'm there in two." He pocketed the phone and flat-out ran, darting past pedestrians and leaping over a small dog tethered to an older man's wrist.

Why hadn't they gone into the restaurant? He had no time to puzzle it out. His boots pounded down the alley, and he almost plowed into Bette as she ran the opposite direction.

"Where's Jane?" he demanded.

She didn't answer. He gripped her shoulders and bent to look her square in the face. It was as if he peered into a long and lonely tunnel. "Where, Bette?"

Bette pointed to the rear lot. "Go inside the restaurant," he told her. "Stay until I come for you."

He clattered on, skidding on a spot slick with oil until he plunged out into the rear lot.

His phone buzzed with a text. I'm at your three o'clock.

He jerked a look to his right and saw Liam sneaking behind a parked car. He would check row by row starting from his end. Mitch began to do the same from the opposite side. Pulse raging, gun drawn, he scooted from fender to fender, both fearing and praying that he would find Jane. But what if it was already too late?

"God, You save her," he muttered savagely. "She trusts You. Make it right." It wasn't so much a prayer as a demand, tossed like a rock with more anger than he'd ever felt in his life. Another row, and there was no Jane, no Wade. Finally Liam scurried to him, bent low, both hands on his gun.

"Nothing," he said.

Desperate, Mitch jumped in the bed of the nearest truck. From his vantage point he caught a glimpse, the tiniest flash of a fender vanishing around the corner of the building.

"East," he thundered.

"My truck's here," Liam said. They ran to his vehicle. Liam peeled out of the lot heading east, but he was forced to wait for a family crossing the road.

When it was clear, he guided the truck to the first intersection.

"Which way?" he said.

Mitch scanned desperately. Left would take them to a winding road that ran along the coast and met up with the highway after it crossed the mountain. To the right was a sleepy small-town street dotted with houses, a shopping area and the Roughwater Lodge.

Which way? Isolation, the lonely beach, dozens of places to pull off behind rocks, deserted spots where Wade would not be interrupted. Bile rose in his throat. But what if he was wrong? Perhaps Wade anticipated that Mitch would follow, figured his brother would come to that very conclusion.

But Driftwood was a small town and people noticed strangers, especially now when word of Wade's actions had started to spread, thanks in part to Barber's presence.

Which way? Left or right? If he made the wrong choice, Jane would die—he felt the truth of that in his bones. Maybe Bette, too. She'd looked so lost in her college shirt and jeans with the hole in the knee.

Liam idled at the light, shoulders tense, head cocked so he would not miss Mitch's decision. Mitch flashed on the faces at the trial, not the photos of the women Wade had murdered, but the real, live mothers, sisters, aunts, left behind to grieve. Their anguished expressions in the courtroom said it all. Why had their women had to die, just because they trusted the wrong man?

And what if Jane dies because she put her trust in that man's brother?

The seconds ticked away like sand trickling through his clenched fingers. Three things, he reminded himself. Wade needed three things—money, communication and a place to stay. He'd found those things somewhere nearby. He might take Jane there, to wherever he was holing up, and wait for dark to get away.

Left or right?

"Left," Mitch said.

The light turned green, and Liam hit the gas.

"God, You save her," he whispered again, only this time he added, "Please."

Jane's head spun as she stared at Wade from the passenger seat.

"Let me go," she tried to say, but her throat was dry as sand, her body dazed.

He drove along a twisting road, edged with precarious black cliffs that plunged down to the ocean. Then he wrenched the car off the road and they bumped and skidded for what seemed like hours, though it was probably not even fifteen minutes, taking a path that grew more sandy and wild the farther they went. She put her hand on the door handle, ready to jump out.

"Don't even try it," he said. He'd slowed the car, edged down a faint trail that looked as though it led directly to the ocean. She realized with sickening certainty that he knew where he was going, that he'd been planning her abduction. At least Bette had gotten away. Jane tried to hang on to the fact that she had not failed Bette a second time. Wade spoke, making her jump.

"Oh, Jane, how could you do it?" He pounded his fist on the steering wheel. "How could you stab a knife in my heart after everything I did for you?"

His face had gone stark with anger, his cheeks two dusky spots. "I don't know what you're talking about. Let me go, Wade. You said you loved me."

He hit the brakes then, so suddenly that her head

snapped forward and the rear of the truck shimmied. She tried to wrench open the door handle, but her fingers refused to cooperate.

He opened the door and hauled her out. She stumbled and fell to her knees. They were alone, concealed by a cage of rocks, the ocean thundering on the other side of the barrier. The grit abraded her knees through the fabric of her jeans. Far away a gull shrieked. No one would see them this far off the road. The isolation slammed her like a fist.

Wade wrapped his arms tight to his body as if trying to contain some strong emotion. "I thought you came to Driftwood because you knew I'd be here, that we could be together after I killed Mitch. I was so certain. You are weak, Jane, but I didn't think you were a traitor."

Jane stared up at him, the sun dazzling her eyes where it shone over the top of the rocks. Bette would get help, she told herself. She'd find Mitch or Liam and tell them what had happened. But had she seen which direction Wade had taken her?

"Wade…"

"Quiet," he snarled. "I can't understand how I could be so wrong. Blinded by my love of you, it must be."

You've never loved anyone but yourself, she thought. She forced her lungs to keep working. "Wade, tell me what's upset you."

He did not appear to hear. "I was wrong, I realize now. You came to Mitch because you wanted me put away again. I could forgive you cooperating with the cops because you are a coward at heart, they threatened and bullied you, no doubt, Mitch was always a brute, but he's stupid, of course, taking you to town, thinking that a public setting would scare me off."

She tried to keep him talking, to buy time. "Tell me what you're so mad about."

His eyes brimmed with hatred, lips quivering with rage. "But what you've done, Jane, Jane…" His hands balled into fists. "I can't forgive you."

"For what?" she begged. "For meeting with Bette?"

He blinked, surprised, and she realized he wasn't thinking about Bette Whipple. He crouched so his face was level with hers, his expression stark and mad. Reaching into his pocket, he pulled out a photo and shoved it inches from her nose.

Her heart turned to glass and shattered into millions of tiny pieces that cut deep. She began to cry.

TWENTY-ONE

Blood pounded in Mitch's temples as Liam rocketed the truck along the road.

"Too far," he said.

Liam hadn't heard him. Mitch clapped him on the shoulder. "Too far. We should have seen him by now."

Liam jerked the truck into a U-turn and drove the opposite direction, slower, Mitch scanning the sandy shoulder of the road, Liam's eyes narrowed on the road ahead.

"There," Mitch shouted.

Liam braked, and they leaped out. It wasn't much to see, just a faint track in the sand where a vehicle had left the road.

He looked at Liam. "Get help. Call Foley."

"Not leaving you."

"Wade's not worth risking your life for."

"You are."

Mitch felt a hitch in his chest. Though his biological family was wrecked beyond repairing, he'd been given a family more precious than gold that no circumstances could tear apart. He didn't deserve it, couldn't earn it, never even asked for it, but he'd been given it. A blessing, Aunt Ginny would say, and at long last he knew she was right.

He answered Liam with a curt nod. Without any further conversation, they both charged down toward the jumbled rocks. Mitch's panic revved into high gear.

Hang on, Jane. Just hang on.

There was a little boy with clear blue eyes waiting back home for her, a child who needed his courageous, faithful mother to walk through this life with him. Jane believed that God would give her a future with her boy, and he wanted with everything in him at that moment to believe the same thing. Wade had destroyed her past but not her future, not if Mitch had breath in his body.

He pushed faster. A sound came from twenty feet away. He signaled to Liam, who nodded and crept around a pile of rocks while Mitch did the same. Mitch pulled his gun. Before he'd made it ten paces, he heard a shout and a gunshot. Energy swamped his body, and he sprinted forward. A second shot mingled with the roar of an engine as a compact car hurtled forward from behind a granite pile, Wade at the wheel. Another car skidded to a stop. Foley jumped out and took a futile shot at Wade's retreating car.

Liam burst from his hiding place, looked at Mitch and then shot a disgusted look at Foley. "I'll go back to the truck, see if I can make out where he's headed."

Foley holstered his weapon. "He heard you coming. You messed up my bust."

Mitch did not trust himself to answer. Instead he scanned the ground, looking for any sign of Jane. She was the only thing that mattered now. Had she been hit? Was she still in Wade's car? Was there even the slightest chance that she'd gotten free? Fear choked off his breathing. Or had Wade killed her and left her for dead in some sandy shallow?

He scanned closer, trying to pick out a clue. Lurching forward, he'd made it two steps when Jane stepped out from between two rocks. His joy turned to terror.

She was scratched and hunched over, her face a white blur in the mottled sunlight, but the look on her face stopped his breathing. She did not appear to notice Foley was there at all. Mitch ran to her, gripping her forearms as she collapsed onto her knees. In her hand she squeezed a crumpled paper so tightly her fingernails dug half-moons into her palm. He saw no signs that she'd been shot, no blood-soaked patches on her clothing.

"Jane," he said, "what did he do to you?"

"Calling for an ambulance," Foley said, speaking into his radio.

"Jane," he continued, stroking her face, chafing her arms, heedless of what Foley might think, desperate to comfort her. She seemed to be unable even to support herself on her knees, so he picked her up.

"Here," Foley called. "Put her in my car."

He followed Foley to his squad car and put her in the back seat. He accepted a blanket from Foley and crouched next to her, stroking her hand, trying to think of the soothing sounds he'd heard her use when Ben had fallen and scraped his knee.

"It's okay. You're safe now," he murmured. "The ambulance is on its way."

She did not cry, but just rocked back and forth. His desperation mounted.

"If you had—" Foley started.

His blood went hot. "If this is an 'I told you so'

right now, Foley, we're gonna have a real serious issue." The dangerous tone must have been persuasive. Foley paused a beat.

"We've been tracking all the contacts, letters written to Wade during his prison time. Plenty of hate mail but one consistent writer. Postmarked from a town called Stottsville. We think it might be the ex-girlfriend. We're tracking her last known whereabouts."

"Think she might be funding him?"

"Makes sense."

He wouldn't admit that he'd been up late each night calling, poking around on Liam's computer, trying every trick he'd ever learned in his days as a marshal to sniff out any source of support Wade might be calling upon. Instead he kept his gaze on Jane, stroking her hands and murmuring.

"How'd you know where Wade was today?" Mitch said over his shoulder.

Foley snorted. "You have to know we have eyes on you, right?"

He did. It was exactly what he would have done in Foley's place.

"So you spotted Bette Whipple?"

"Yeah, and that was all kinds of crazy for her to come to Driftwood."

"She's scared. Wade has that effect on people. Can you help her?"

"If we can find her. Maybe she will have the good sense to listen to us."

He was about to fire off an angry retort when Jane sucked in a shuddering breath and blinked.

"I have to get back. I have to…" Her breathing grew so rapid he was afraid she might hyperventilate.

"The ambulance is almost here…"

"No," she squeezed out. "I have to get back, right now." She was struggling to get out of the car, to push past him as if she would run down the road in the direction of town. He grabbed her arm to stop her. She twirled around so quickly she almost fell.

"Jane," he said. "You need to stay here, to get checked out by the medics."

She thrust the piece of paper at him. It was a photo, balled and creased, of Ben, walking between Jane and Mitch, his little legs almost lost in the tall green grass of Roughwater Ranch. "Wade gave it to me," she whispered. "He knows."

Mitch's vision narrowed for a moment, his fear and anger coalescing into one dark spot. From far away he heard Foley say, "So it's true, then. She does have a son—Wade's son."

"No," Jane snapped in a voice hard as diamond. "Ben is *my* son, and Wade's not going to get him, ever."

Mitch put a hand on her back, the other gripping his phone. He sent a frantic text to the ranch. "We'll go right now."

"I'll dispatch Patron, too," Foley said.

He did not add what Mitch knew he was thinking. *And we'll take both of you into custody like we should have in the first place.* Something ticked under Mitch's consciousness, a piece he could not see the edges of as he supported Jane back to the truck. There was no time to do anything but drive as fast as he could back to Roughwater Ranch.

Jane knew she would have been dead if Wade hadn't been interrupted. She could not summon up the emotional energy to care. All that mattered was getting to her son.

The phone rang, and Mitch banged the speaker button.

"Ben's fine," Uncle Gus said. "We're locked in. Danny Patron is patrolling the property. Tell Jane her boy is safe."

She almost started sobbing at the last word. *He's okay.* She repeated it over and over in her mind.

Mitch drove to the edge of reckless, but not quite over. "Breathe," he told her. "Breathe slow."

The words did not penetrate deep down. Wade's face blotted all other thoughts away.

But what you've done, Jane... I can't forgive you.

She was out of the truck before it had fully stopped.

"Jane," he shouted, but she paid no mind, running to the front door, which was flung open by Aunt Ginny.

"It's okay," she called. "Ben's fine."

Jane ran past her, flew through the foyer and into the living room, where Ben sat on his splayed knees, playing with the train Mitch had given him. Her cry startled him and sent Catty Cat running under the nearest chair.

"Mommy?" he said as if he didn't recognize her.

She gathered him up and held him, smelled him, touched him, prayed to God with thanks he was safe, until he squirmed and she loosened her grip. "Ben Bear," she said.

He scooted away. "Mommy, owie?" He put up a tiny finger near her face but did not touch her. She could not answer for the tears clogging her throat.

Mitch knelt gently on one knee. "Yes," he said to Ben. "Mommy got an owie, but we'll fix it up, okay?"

He took her hand and started to lead her away, but she resisted.

"I'm staying with Ben," she said.

He bent low and murmured in her ear. "Honey, Ben is okay. Liam's here, and Danny. We need to take care of you now, just for a minute. Ben's…not used to seeing you hurt."

She realized what Mitch was trying to say, that she'd scared her son, her fear overflowing and turning her into someone he did not recognize. It sent a knife blade right through her. "I'll be right back, Ben," she choked out. Blinking back tears, she followed Mitch into the guest room and sank down onto the bed, struggling to keep the sobs in check.

He closed the door and went to the bathroom, returning with a first-aid kit. Squirting some disinfectant onto a cotton ball, he gently dabbed at her cuts. It stung, but nothing close to the agony she felt inside.

"He's going to come," she said. "He's going to come for his son."

Mitch finished tending to her cuts and sat on a chair. "Yes," he said.

"What should I do?"

He looked at his knees, got up and paced back and forth. "I think it's time to do as Foley says."

She felt like she'd been struck. "Do you trust him?"

"Not completely, but he's following the same leads I would have. I would let some former colleagues know the situation, just to be sure there are more ears involved. The marshals can move you from here, settle you somewhere until…"

"Until when? Until they capture Wade? If they ever

do?" She shook her head. "You and I both know Wade will never give up."

"Jane, I don't want it to be like this."

"Yes, you do," she shouted, the fury and rage splashing out in a rush. "You've given up and you want to hand us over."

He spun to face her. "That's not true."

"Yes, it is. You are afraid to face your brother and you'll abandon us."

He stepped closer, a flash of anger on his face. "Look at me."

She couldn't. Instead she pounded her fists on her thighs in frustration. "I can't love you and that's what you want, so you'll surrender us. If you can't have us, no one will, just like your brother."

He recoiled as if she'd slapped him. Then he squared his shoulders. "You don't have to believe it," he said, "but I would rather take a bullet than let any harm come to you and Ben, and I think deep down you know that."

And she did. She bit her lip, tears running down her cheeks, mortified at what she'd said, at how she'd cut at him with the very sharpest words she could muster. *I'm sorry*, she wanted to say, but she could not get her mouth to do it through her chattering teeth. He led her to a rocking chair she had not noticed, guiding her into it and wrapping a blanket around her.

"This chair. It wasn't here before."

He tucked the blanket tighter. "Just an old glider rocker from a thrift store. Painted it up nice. Thought maybe Ben wasn't too old for rocking. I...uh...probably shouldn't have put it here, in light of...everything."

In light of the fact that she'd shredded his heart. She

simply could not reply, clamping her jaws tight together to hold in the ricocheting emotions.

"We'll need to talk to Foley," he said in a gentle tone. She wished he'd had some steel in it, some anger, which she deserved, but she could not weaken, could not be soft, not with her child's fate in the balance.

"I will tell him what I decide," she said, stressing the pronoun. She knew it was cruel, and he did not deserve it. But he'd as much as said he would not help her any more, and surrendering herself to the marshals could not be her only option. Surrender itself must never be her choice.

Mitch walked silently to the door and closed it behind him without looking back.

Slowly, she rocked in the chair, trying to soothe herself with the motion. For the briefest of moments she'd allowed herself to imagine that maybe God had a plan for her and her son here in Driftwood, to put down the most fragile beginnings of roots. Her desperate longing for a town that might be home to Ben, with a man who could be a rock for her and her son, was all just a dream.

She considered her reflection in the mirror, bloodied, bruised, defeated. She'd been wrong. Mitch could not protect her, and the sleepy little town could not be the sanctuary she'd craved.

She had only one remaining choice.

Run as far from Roughwater Ranch as she could.

TWENTY-TWO

Mitch sat down at the table with sick certainty in his stomach. He tried to shove aside the memories of what had just transpired with Jane. Foley sipped coffee and waited, a self-satisfied smile hovering around his mouth. On the carpet Liam played with Ben, building a complex tower and demolishing it. Mitch wasn't sure who enjoyed the wrecking more, Liam or Ben.

When Ben wearied of the game, he rubbed his eyes and looked across the room right at Mitch. "'Nack, Uncle Moo Moo?"

Liam stared in puzzlement. "He wants a snack," Mitch translated.

Liam cocked a grin at him. "You've learned to speak toddler, Uncle Moo Moo. Well done."

Mitch held out his hand to Ben, who scooped up Catty Cat, wandered over and held out his hands. Mitch shifted. "Uh…"

"He wants you to pick him up," Liam said with a laugh. "I guess you haven't mastered the toddler nonverbal yet, Moo."

Mitch reached down, and Ben climbed into his arms. He carried him into the kitchen, marveling at the feather-

weight bundle of boy. So small, so perfect, so filled
with love and curiosity. Ben snuggled, leaning his head
against Mitch's chest. He was humming something about
horses.

Mitch sat him at the table. "What would you like to
eat, Ben?"

"Cookies?"

"Does Mommy let you have cookies before lunch?"

Ben nodded earnestly, and Mitch had to laugh. "I have
an idea." He stuck a piece of bread in the toaster. When
it popped out, he added a coating of butter and a tiny
sprinkle of sugar and cinnamon. He figured it had less
bad stuff than a cookie. Before he handed it to Ben, he
took a knife and cut the bread into a rough horse shape.

Ben's eyes rounded as he slid the snack in front of
him. "Horse."

"Yes," Mitch said, ridiculously pleased that Ben was
impressed with his crude bread carving.

"Catty Cat, too?"

"I don't think cats eat toast." But he found a bowl and
poured a splash of milk in it for the kitten.

Ben folded his hands and waited for Mitch to do the
same. It took Mitch a moment to figure out praying was
in order. Then Ben bowed his head and said, "Tank you,
Father, for the 'nack."

The words sent an arrow straight to Mitch's core.
So simple, a thank-you from a child fathered by an evil
man and still so full of love he just about brimmed over
with it. Mitch found it hard to breathe. Something inside him was twisting and morphing like molten steel
on the blacksmith's anvil. The beauty of Ben's simple
trust mirrored his mother's and peeled away Mitch's
inner seal with fiery intensity. Ben's God, Jane's God,

could be his God, too. The notion dizzied him. This love, the downright opposite of evil, could be his, if he managed to turn away from his blistered past. The goodness spread in front of him like a feast, and the thought of partaking undid him.

He was grateful that Ben did not seem to mind his silence, munching at the toast and drinking milk that left him with a white mustache. All of a sudden, the child jerked a look toward the window.

Mitch followed his gaze to find a peregrine falcon soaring over the ranch, wings spread in feathered splendor. Mitch scooped Ben up and they both stood at the glass, admiring the majestic path of the bird as it glided over the windswept pastures.

"Birdie," Ben said, sticky hands cupping Mitch's cheeks in excitement.

"That's a falcon, Ben," he said, in awe of the sheer joy he felt at sharing time with the boy.

"Ohhh," Ben said. "Falcon."

"That's right." Something trickled through Mitch's mind. The detail floated on the edges of his grasp as Ben reached up and gently patted the scar on his cheek.

His eyes were somber. He peered into Mitch's face and skimmed his fingertips over the puckered flesh. "Owie?"

Mitch cleared his throat. "Yes, that's an owie."

With concentrated effort, Ben kissed the tip of his finger and pressed it to Mitch's scar, like he'd seen his mother do. Mitch's vision went fuzzy with tears, and he gulped. How he loved this boy…and his mother.

"All better?" Ben asked.

"Yes," he managed. "All better."

With his breath still hitched in his throat, he wiped Ben's hands and went to find Jane. He could not deci-

pher the expression on her face, and he hoped his own
wasn't too fogged from the precious moments he'd spent
with Ben. "He was hungry. I fixed him a snack."

"Thank you," she said without meeting Mitch's eyes.
"I'll just put him down for a nap." She emerged from
her room a short time later, composed, he guessed, from
whatever decision she'd come to.

Foley pushed his coffee cup away at her approach.
"I'm sorry for what happened today," he said. "And I
understand why you didn't want to make it public that
you have Wade's son."

Jane's jaw clenched.

"I'm sorry. I know Ben is your son." He lifted a
shoulder. "But you get it now, right? There's no way to
ensure your safety or his unless we bring you in." His
look drifted to Mitch. "Mitch had things go his way
once when he put Wade behind bars, but not this time.
He can't help you. I can."

Mitch watched, dread coursing through him. He
knew what her answer should be and understood it
meant he would likely never see her or Ben again. It
was justified—he'd failed her, and what was more, he'd
fallen in love with her and her son, which only added
to her burdens. For that, he would not forgive himself,
and he would try with all his might not to make it any
harder than it had to be.

Foley straightened. "My phone, sorry." His mouth
tightened as he listened. "On my way." He disconnected. "That was Patron. He says they've spotted the
car Wade was driving near a motel in Copper Top."

"That's twenty miles from here," Mitch informed
Jane. Though he wanted to hope, to believe that this

might possibly be the end, he could not bring himself to credit it.

"I've gotta go," Foley said. "I'll call you when I know something. In the meantime, I'll get an officer posted nearby to keep eyes on the ranch. Wade won't make a move, because he knows folks are armed around here."

"That's certain," Uncle Gus said. "And we decide who gets past the gate and who doesn't."

Liam nodded his silent-lipped agreement.

"And Chad's gone up to the tower to take a turn at watch," Aunt Ginny added. "It's not a proper castle," she said with a smile at Jane, "just a room I use for my office, but it's got almost a 360-degree view of the property. If anyone comes, Chad will know, and he's an excellent shot, so…"

Jane worried her lower lip between her teeth. "But the photo…" she said. "It was taken at the ranch."

"At long range with a telephoto lens," Foley finished.

Which implied an expensive camera… A thought snapped into place.

Mitch waited until Foley left. "I have to go check on something."

"You need me to come?" Liam said.

"No, need you here. Chad, too."

Liam frowned, but he didn't object.

Mitch turned to Jane. "I can't tell you what decision to make, but please stay here until I get back."

She tilted her head, and he knew. She was going to run. Having felt the weight of a child against his heart, seen the pure trust in Ben's blue eyes, he figured he finally understood why she would risk everything, every last thing including her own life, to save Ben's. Sacrifice like that could only be a divine thing. He got it. He finally got it.

He pressed a kiss to her temple. "Please," he said. "Please be here when I get back."

She didn't answer. He had a chance, a slim shot to make things right—not because of guilt, but because of love.

Jane stayed with Ben, reading books, playing with the train Mitch had made him, watching from the window to see some of the hands coming and going from their pasture duties. They were all trusted members of the extended Whitehorse clan. She knew they were aware of the reputation she brought, the hatred she'd awakened in some of the townspeople, but she'd felt nothing from them but quiet support. If Aunt Ginny, Gus, Liam and Mitch vouched for Jane, that was good enough.

She relived the last moment with Mitch. *Please... please be here when I get back.* How she wanted to, how her heart longed to settle into the warm comfort of his care, his devotion and love, which he'd offered but she could not accept. Loving him meant staying, trusting, allowing her future and her son's to rest squarely in the hands of another man, another Whitehorse. As much as she craved it, she knew she must not allow it.

Ben lay down across her lap and cuddled with Catty Cat. Helen arrived and joined them, chatting about nothing in particular. Jane appreciated the distraction, easing the minutes along as they ticked closer to her departure. Darkness would be her only help.

Aunt Ginny approached and handed her the house phone. "It's a call for you," she said. For a fleeting moment, Jane's heart leaped at the thought that it might be

Mitch or Foley with news that would restore her future. She gripped the phone.

"Jane?"

She heaved out a breath of both relief and disappointment. "Bette. Are you okay? I've been so worried about you." Jane nodded to Helen, who was starting in on a rousing game of blocks with Ben under the kitten's close supervision.

She moved to the guest room, clutching the phone tight. "Where are you?"

"In my car. I've been sleeping in it, moving around some, trying to decide what to do. I heard in town—I mean, I heard he took you, but you got away. I'm glad. I didn't mean for you to get hurt."

"Oh, Bette. Do you think Wade saw you?"

"No, no, I'm pretty sure."

"Then you can get away. Even if he did spot you, it's okay. He…he's after me."

"But he told me no one gets to leave him, ever. He said we were 'his women.'" Jane heard the quiver in Bette's voice. "I thought, I mean, your letter was so nice. Remember what you said in it?"

She did, the tearstained words she'd labored over for hours.

I would do anything to be able to go back and make it right, to hear and notice and see what Wade was doing, to free you from that underground room. Since I can't do that, I want you to know that if I ever have the opportunity, I will help you in any way I can. In the meantime, I will pray for you.

Bette's words snapped her back to the present. "I don't have anybody. I got married young, at eighteen, but my husband left me right after I got my nursing degree. That was a year before Wade. After, I mean, I tried to go back to nursing, but I couldn't concentrate anymore. I tried to reenroll in college for my master's, to make new friends, but I couldn't seem to restart my life."

"I understand." Jane wished she could reach through the connection and hold Bette's hand, help her like she'd promised.

"You're the only one in the world who can, I guess." Bette sniffed. "What are you going to do?"

She fell silent for a moment. When she didn't answer, Bette spoke up.

"You can come with me. I have an apartment in SoCal. We can share it, watch each other's backs."

Jane blinked back tears. "I can't."

Bette's voice sharpened. "I get it. You've got other people, and you don't need me."

"It's not that. Wade is coming after me, and no one is safe if I'm nearby."

Bette let out a long, low sigh. "Okay. It would have been nice, though, to have a friend."

"It's not too late for you," Jane said. "Get your master's or find a job you love—the friends will fall into place. I'm sure of it."

"So weird that you would be offering me advice," Bette said. "But I'm grateful. You must be some kind of lady to be Wade's ex-wife."

Jane felt the tears flow down her face for this lost soul. Though she had survived her encounter with Wade, she was still imprisoned by him. Before she had time to reconsider, she gave Bette her cell number.

"I don't know when I'll be able to settle somewhere," Jane said, "but we can be in touch someday. You can tell me when you've restarted your life, okay?"

"You're going to run, aren't you?"

"Best if you don't know my plans."

"All right. I guess I'd better go."

"Me, too. God bless, Bette."

But she had already disconnected.

TWENTY-THREE

Mitch called Elaine Barber's number on the back of the card she'd given him. No answer, so he left a message.

"We have to talk. Now."

She had access to the town, she'd known where Nana Jo and Ben had been staying, and she had a real nice camera. What better person to be feeding information to Wade? He should have guessed before that she might be the one who had been sending letters to Wade in prison and now she was his support, his home base. It had taken only one phone call to the *West Coast Bee* to discover they'd never heard of an Elaine Barber.

Rusty, Mitch. He prowled the town, looking for Barber, poking his head into the coffee shop, the hardware store. He finally pulled up at the gas station, where Eddie polished the pumps. Eddie had retired from his work as a health inspector, and he channeled all his energy into the station he'd bought a decade back—Eddie's gas station was cleaner than some restaurants where Mitch had eaten. Eddie removed his sun hat and listened, rubbing his speckled bald head.

"Saw her this morning. She filled up early, just like last week."

"Last week? She's filled up twice in that time?"

"Yes." He nodded. "Asked about your kin, too."

Mitch blew out a breath. "Everybody wants to know about Wade."

"Not Wade."

Nerves fired along Mitch's extremities, lifting the hairs on his arms. "Who?"

"Your pops."

He nodded thanks and ran to his truck, dialing his father's number as he went.

One ring. Two, three, no answer.

He could be out for a walk, fishing, making a run to the hardware store, anyplace. But the mantra rolled through Mitch's mind.

Three things…money, communication, a base of operations. Wade could secure all three of those things at Pops's place, especially with Elaine Barber's help.

He could make it to his father's by truck, but it would be faster on horseback. The stop at the ranch took only a few minutes, and though he waved to Chad up in the tower, he did not slow to give a report. He knew Liam, Chad and Gus would insist on coming with him. It would not do. He wanted all their guns ready for Wade if he showed up, and besides, if anything happened to any of them trying to bring down his brother… No. Wade would not have anyone else. No more victims. Not this time or any time. It would end today.

He messaged Foley, who didn't answer his phone, urged Rosie to a trot as he found the head of the trail that bisected the pastureland, aiming directly for the coast. The morning sun had blossomed earlier but had been replaced by an oppressive gray cloud cover. Rosie moved easily up the trail, her strong flanks taking the slope in stride. Like the good horse she was, she sensed his urgency, and by the time they reached the sloping part of the trail, she was galloping, the wind catching her mane. He leaned low and let her have her way, his gut churning with everything in him.

As they clattered over the rocky ground and reached sea level, he saw Barber's car parked on the edge of the dock. He slid off Rosie, leaving her loose, and sprinted to his father's slip as quietly as he could, plastered against the cabin door. Bobbing his head up, he risked a look through the tiny window. He saw no one, but his glance had taken in an important detail—there was a pizza box open on the wooden table. Pops had never learned to like pizza, and the thrifty man would never have indulged in an extravagance for himself anyway.

There was no time to wait for police or marshals or anyone else. He might be too late now to save his father's life. He counted to three and charged in. His heart stopped.

There were two bodies on the floor. Everything in him wanted to render aid, but the cop instincts were in full fire. He quickly checked from bow to stern and below until he confirmed there was no one hiding. Then he called for an ambulance, dropped the phone and gently rolled his father over. Blood stained his temple, and to Mitch's great elation, he moaned.

"Pops, don't worry," he breathed. "Ambulance is on its way." He put his father on his side, draped a blanket over him and went to the second victim.

His mind struggled to comprehend as he rolled Elaine Barber onto her back. She too was breathing, but bleeding heavily from a stab wound in her side. At first he'd thought perhaps Pops had defended himself, but this sizable entry point was not the work of any of Pops's knives.

He grabbed a clean towel from the drawer and applied pressure to the wound. The gleam of a chain around her neck drew his attention, and he pulled out a badge, spattered with blood—a badge he knew well.

US marshal.

He pulled her phone from her pocket and used her thumb to unlock it. Foley's number was the first in her contacts. Foley had put a team into place, and Elaine Barber had been watching Pops's place as a good agent should. Mitch guessed she'd tried to take Wade down and he'd won the contest.

He put the phone on the floor and hit the speaker button. Foley's phone rang once, twice. When Foley answered, Mitch barked into the phone. "You've got an agent down at my father's place, bleeding bad. Go pick up Jane and Ben. I'll stay until an ambulance arrives."

"Mitch..." Foley started.

He cut through the reply. "Did you get Wade?"

"No."

"Then you have to take Jane and Ben into custody. Right now. By whatever means necessary."

"Copy that," Foley said. "Take care of Barber. She's a good cop. I'll send backup."

He took three precious seconds to tap out a text to Jane on his phone. Go with Foley.

The towel was now soaked crimson, and he could do nothing but press both hands to Barber's side and pray that Wade had not taken another woman's life.

Jane answered her cell phone. "I'm coming over as soon as I get clear of this briefing to take you and your son into protective custody," Foley said.

"No," Jane said, "I..."

"Mitch just called me. He said to do it now. I'll be there within the hour."

"I…"

"Listen, lady. If you don't come, I'll leak this story to every wire service in the country. Everyone will know Jane Whitehorse is holing up at the Roughwater Ranch. Their mailbox will overflow with hate letters."

"You can't do that."

"I can, and what's more, Mitch will approve. He said to take whatever means necessary. Be ready in an hour. I had to reroute the cop I had stationed at the ranch, so stay put."

Her heart quaked. Mitch? Mitch had stripped her of her right to choose for her son? In spite of his mistrust of Foley, he would hand her over to him? And Ben?

She was back again in the moment when she'd realized it was all true—Wade, the man she'd trusted to be her life partner, had been the worst mistake of her life.

And now, it seemed, she'd made the same mistake again. It burned like fire when she pictured Mitch, his dark eyes, the rare smile, the man of honor she'd thought him to be, the manipulation she'd fallen for. He'd decided to turn her over, to sacrifice her and Ben.

The betrayal scalded.

The shock swamped her soul.

But what hurt most, deep down, was the fact that she realized that she'd almost allowed herself to fall in love with Wade's brother, and she'd given him permission to hurt her, too.

But not her son.

She could still keep Ben safe.

Through tears, she picked up her phone and called for a taxi. Then she went to tell the family that she would be taking her son away immediately.

TWENTY-FOUR

As he strained to hear signs of an emergency response vehicle, Mitch mulled over his mistake. His father had begun to rouse.

"Pops," he called. "Pops, it's Mitch."

"Wade was here," Pops mumbled.

"I know. I'm sorry I wasn't able to stop him."

"He told me he's going to take his son back." A tear rolled down his father's bruised cheek. "I'm too weak, too old. I couldn't stand up to him."

Mitch swallowed hard. "Not your fault, Pops."

"The child… Is he safe? Is Jane?"

He couldn't answer.

"I'm praying," he said, eyes closed, lips quivering.

Me, too, Mitch said silently, praying for the woman bleeding in his care, and the one who was painfully out of reach.

Liam, Chad, Gus, Helen and Ginny stood in the foyer as she shouldered the small bag Ginny had given her, now stuffed with new muffins and pieces of plastic-wrapped pie, as well as the toys Helen insisted that Ben keep. Ben stood at her knee, sobbing.

"Don't worry," Aunt Ginny said. "We'll take great care of Catty Cat, and when you come back, you can play with him." She kissed Ben's head.

Liam said what they were all thinking, she imagined. "Stay here. At least until we hear from Mitch."

"I already heard from Mitch. He wants me to go with Foley. If I don't, Foley will leak that I'm here and I'll have to go anyway. This way I decide where and when."

"But…"

She held up a hand. "You have all been nothing but kind to me, but I have to know that I'm still making the choices for Ben. He's all that matters."

Uncle Gus cleared his throat. "At least let one of us escort you…until you get settled."

Jane smiled and kissed his cheek. "No," she said firmly. "But thank you."

He reached for his wallet. "Well, you'll need some money."

She shook her head. "We still have some from the sale of my shop in the bank. Enough to last a little while. I'll be okay. We'll be okay." She wished she could own the bravado she forced into the words. After kissing each one of them and clasping Ginny in a hug, she let herself out the front door and into the waiting taxi.

Chad had already strapped the car seat into the rear, and she let Ben look back one more time and wave to the group gathered at the front door. He was still crying when she strapped him in.

"Where to?" the cabbie said.

"To the bus station, but not the one here in town. There's one an hour north of here, right, in Ridgeway?"

"Well, sure, but you can just hop onto a bus here in town…"

"Ridgeway," she said firmly.

"Yes, ma'am," he said.

She settled back in the seat and checked her phone again. There had been no further word from Mitch or Foley.

Whip up or whoa, she thought.

Through the thick lump in her throat, she forced out a breath. Time to whip up and get away while she still could.

She leaned back in the seat and tried to close her eyes. It might be the last hour she'd have to nap for a while. She heard the cabbie's sharp surprised breath and something slammed hard into the cab, knocking it off the road. She flung a hand out toward Ben, but the car toppled over. Her head smacked into the side door, and the world went black.

Elaine Barber somehow managed to survive, and the medics took over, working frantically to get her stabilized for transport on a helicopter. Mitch's father was already being loaded into an ambulance, his pulse steady, his breathing strong. The cop Foley had sent was securing the scene, photographing every square inch inside and out of the boat.

"Here," a medic said, giving him some wipes to cleanse his hands.

He did so absently, details and facts rolling over in his mind.

"You saved her life, you know," the medic said. "She would have bled out if you hadn't found her in time." Over his shoulder, a bird skimmed the cliffs.

He froze, ignoring the medic's comment. Falcon. The image stuck in his mind, him and Ben admiring

the majestic bird. Falcon, emblazoned on Bette's yellow
T-shirt. The Fighting Falcons...the mascot of a South-
ern California college football team.

He pulled out his phone and typed into the search
bar.

He heard Foley saying it again. *We've been track-*
ing all the contacts, letters written to Wade during his
prison time. Plenty of hate mail, but one consistent
writer. Postmarked from a town called Stottsville.

But Bette was Wade's victim...wasn't she?

Finally the phone supplied the answer. The Fighting Falcons were the home team of a small college in
Stottsville, California. He knew deep in his gut that
Bette Whipple was the one who had been writing letters to Wade in prison, the one who had probably helped
him track Jane to Nana Jo's, and for whatever reason,
she was determined to hand Jane over to her psycho
ex-husband.

He bolted to Rosie and they galloped away, leaving
the openmouthed medic standing on the dock.

Jane awakened slowly, a dull ringing sounding in
her ears. Her nerves jerked into motion with one terrified thought.

Ben!

She was somehow on her knees on the grass, someone tugging at her arm. Blinking, she saw the upside-
down cab, the driver feebly moving in the front seat.
Ben, her heart cried again, and she lurched to her feet,
realizing that someone was tugging at her arm, helping her along.

It was Bette, clutching a crying Ben on one hip and
yanking Jane with the other arm.

"Hurry," she said. "We have to go now. Before they find us."

Brain buzzing, limbs aching, she stumbled along, arriving at a car with a crunched front fender.

"You…you hit the cabbie?" Jane mumbled.

"Get in, quick."

She found herself tumbled into the back seat. Bette handed Ben into her arms and took off, the car lurching along at breakneck speed. Jane could do nothing but hold Ben close.

"Where are you taking us? What is happening?"

Bette smiled brightly in the rearview mirror. "We're taking Ben back to his father."

Jane's blood ran cold. "What? Bette, what are you doing?"

Bette shot her a look in the mirror. "Wade and I are together," she said with a smile. "I realized that he was the only man who really loved me."

"No," Jane said in horror. "No, no."

"At first I didn't think so, but after he went to prison, I wrote him. He explained that I was special. That's why he let me get away. He knew we'd be together someday. I helped him escape from prison, you know, with a spike stick on the road." She giggled. "Easier than I thought."

Jane tried to gather her wits. "Bette, listen to me. Wade doesn't love you. He's manipulating you."

"You can't keep him for yourself, Jane. He asked me to help him kill his brother, and then you showed up and I was scared for a while. I thought he'd dump me for you, the wifey." Her eyes narrowed. "But I helped him a lot, with money and a hotel, even got a box out of storage for him with his granddad's gun. When my money ran out, he didn't get rid of me, Jane. Do you hear? He kept me. That tells you something, doesn't it? We went to his father's house and took what we needed—food and the old man's phone."

She frowned. "He had to stab the woman who barged in. Turns out she was a cop of some sort." She shook her head. "It wasn't Wade's fault, though. He didn't have a choice when she pulled her weapon."

Jane bit her lip to keep from crying out. *Oh, Bette. What have you done?*

"Looking back on it, maybe I shouldn't have handed him the picture I took of your kid, but that worked out well, too. Now he wants you dead. Don't worry, though," she said. "I'll raise Ben as my own. He won't even remember you after a while. He's still young enough."

Jane searched desperately around the car. What could she use to overpower Bette? To escape? She couldn't jump out at this speed without hurting Ben.

"There he is," Bette cooed.

Jane looked through the dusty front windshield at the man standing on the side of the road. She didn't need to see him close-up to know that the smile was in place, the cool, satisfied quirk of the mouth below flat, soulless eyes.

Wade Whitehorse stood waiting for her. No, he didn't value her life at all, she corrected.

He stood waiting for her son.

TWENTY-FIVE

Chad kept his briefing quick as he waited for Liam to saddle up. Rosie shifted under Mitch's weight, amped from their gallop back from Pops's place. "I followed the cab," Chad said, "even though she waved us off. Two miles from here along the frontage road, it was hit by another driver. Minimal damage to car, woman driver. By the time I made it down there, they were moving, continuing south on the frontage road."

Uncle Gus scampered up, followed by Aunt Ginny. "Danny's on scene. The taxi driver is okay, but the response vehicles are still blocking the road."

Giving Wade and Bette more time to abduct Jane and Ben. His teeth were grinding together so hard he had to make a conscious effort to talk.

Liam swung up onto his horse. "Plan?"

"We ride. Chad and Uncle Gus go around in the truck to see if they can stop them before they reach the highway. Foley is rolling also, so be cautious. Don't confront Wade." *Leave that to me.* "Just detain him if you can."

Liam crammed on his hat. "And you and me are gonna ride in like John Wayne?"

Mitch was already urging Rosie toward the gate. "Got a problem with that?"

"No way, boss," he called. "That's just the way I like it."

On horseback, they were able to make their own path, bisecting the green hillsides and cutting a direct path to the main road. From their elevated position they caught sight of the car, stopped in the road where a man stood in a black jacket and jeans, relaxed, waiting. Every muscle in Mitch's body snapped tight.

I'm coming for you, Wade. You won't hurt Jane or Ben. Not gonna happen, not this time.

Liam understood Mitch's pointed finger. He wheeled his horse and galloped ahead. They would come at Wade from two different sides.

The wind roared around him, and Rosie's hooves thundered against the ground as they charged toward Wade.

Jane sat in the car, clutching her son, staring through the dusty windshield at Wade. Bette had slowed almost to a stop.

"Bette," she said, in one last effort. "Listen to me. Wade is manipulating you. He doesn't love you. This…" She tried to keep the pleading out of her voice. "This isn't what love looks like."

What did it look like instead? It came in the form of a huge man crouching low to play toy horses with a little child. It looked like one person risking their comfort and safety to help another. It appeared in the words *I'm sorry* and rang in hard-won laughter drifting up to a starlit sky. "Love is wanting more for the other person than you do for yourself," she choked out.

Bette thought for a long moment, and Jane felt the faint stirring of hope. All Bette had to do was push the gas pedal, drive right past Wade and away from his twisted power. "Wade's close enough for me," Bette said, edging the car forward.

Jane had only a split second. She had one last decision to make, and she prayed God would give her the strength. Holding Ben tightly, she wrenched open the car door and tumbled out before Bette could gain much speed. She hit the ground, arms shielding her son, and rolled once. Then she was on her feet. She heard Bette call out to Wade, but she did not stop, sprinting toward the field, ducking under the wooden rails and through to the pastures. She remembered what Mitch had told her about cattle, that they were basically fourteen hundred pounds of unpredictable animal. She would take her chances with the beasts in front of her instead of the one closing in from behind.

Ben began to cry. "It's okay," she panted. If she could cross through the pasture, maybe she would run into someone from the ranch, or a clump of trees to hide in, something.

Her heart pounded mercilessly against her ribs. *Run, run, run*, her instincts shrieked, but it was slow going with a toddler almost choking her.

When she finally had to stop to catch her breath, she found she was in a small dip of land where there was a watering tank and several dozen full-size cows, regarding her with suspicion. Surrounding them were acres and acres of wide-open range and not a solitary person anywhere.

Frantically, she turned in a circle. Which way? The late-morning sun was prying through the clouds, so she knew which direction was east. Roughwater Ranch would be west, set along the cliffs. *Keep going.* Run back toward the ranch, toward people, her only chance of saving Ben.

She had just turned to go when she felt him behind her.

"Janey," Wade said. "Are you showing my son the ranch? Turn around and let me see my boy."

Hardly able to draw breath, terror screaming in every bone and sinew, she slowly shifted to face him.

"What's your name, son?" Wade said.

Ben didn't answer, stuffing his fingers in his mouth and shrinking back into Jane's shoulder. Wade looked at Jane. "He's mine, anyway. I'll pick out what I want to call him." He held out his palms. "Give him to me."

She recoiled, stepping back until her knees banged against the watering tank. "No, I won't."

"I will take him, Janey, or you can hand him to me. Make it easy so he won't cry anymore." Wade's nose wrinkled. "It's making the snot run down his face."

She summoned every last shred of courage. "Wade, you don't own me, and you don't own Ben. He's my son and I will fight you with my dying breath. You will not take him from me."

Wade tipped back his head and laughed. "Janey, of all the women I have killed, you will always be the best of the bunch."

"Mommy," Ben screamed as Wade marched toward them. Jane turned and ran, clutching her boy, willing her legs to go faster, despairing as she heard Wade closing the gap behind them.

Liam and Mitch burst into the hollow at the same moment. Wade wheeled around and fired. The shot whistled over Mitch's left shoulder.

Jane screamed and cradled Ben to her. Had they been hit?

"Get them out of here," he yelled to Liam, leaping from Rosie and giving her a smack on the rump that sent her galloping away. He tumbled as he hit the ground. Cattle, frightened at the gunshots, ran in a tornado of hooves.

"Liam," he yelled again, unable to see from his belly-down position if Jane and Ben were clear of the stampeding cattle. He used the commotion to roll to his feet.

Wade was scanning for him, had not yet pinned down his position. Mitch knew he had only a moment, and he did not hesitate. Scrambling up, he ran behind the nearest cow, using it as a screen until he got close enough. With a mighty gulp of air, he dived for his brother, with all the vigor and enthusiasm he'd had as a high school tackle. His head made contact with Wade's stomach, the air whooshing out of him. They somersaulted three times. Wade still gripped the gun, and it took all Mitch's energy to clutch at his brother's wrist.

The grass soaked into his back as Wade twisted on top of him.

"I will kill you, brother," he grunted, the whites of his eyes going bloodshot with the effort. "And then I will have my son."

"Not in this lifetime," Mitch choked out, and with a strength he could not have fathomed from his almost forty-year-old self, he squeezed his brother's hand until he heard the bone snap. Wade jerked, and Mitch wrenched the gun free, toppling Wade over backward.

Wade crab walked, blood streaking his face, breathing hard.

They both heard sirens now, and Mitch smiled.

"Don't worry. I'm sure they saved your old room in prison for you."

Wade glowered, beaming hatred as he got to his feet. Mitch raised his weapon. "You won't shoot me," Wade said.

From the corner of his eye, he saw Foley inching closer, hands gripping his weapon. Wade edged backward, limping away toward the road. Mitch lowered his revolver and nodded at Foley. He would allow Foley to have the satisfaction of bringing in the fugitive who had escaped on his watch. This time the arrest and credit would go to Foley.

Foley gave a slight nod, the merest bob of his chin, as much thanks as he would ever show. Mitch didn't care. Foley could have all the kudos he could collect as long as Jane and Ben were safe.

He holstered his gun and ignored the pain rippling through his back and ribs. Down the road, safely sequestered behind Danny Patron's police car, he found Liam.

"Are they...?"

"See for yourself." Liam pointed to the back seat.

Jane erupted from the car, Ben still sheltered in her arms. He blinked hard as she hurtled into his arms. Hands skimming her back, kissing her hair, murmuring silly nothings to Ben, he allowed himself to believe that God had delivered. Jane and Ben were safe.

He tried to speak, but his throat was locked shut. All he could do was hold her and Ben next to his heart and thank God.

TWENTY-SIX

Jane slept for a solid day, awakening in the comfortable guest bed at the Roughwater Ranch only long enough to eat and check on Ben, who was happily taking turns playing with Liam, Chad, Helen and Uncle Gus. The day passed with endless rounds of police interviews and doctor's checks for her and Ben.

As the day wore on, she felt ripples of horror when she considered Bette, who was now in custody. She knew Bette was just another victim, and maybe she and Bette were not so different deep down. Bette could not trust herself to pursue a normal, healthy relationship. She hoped the woman could get some help.

And what about Jane's own self-doubt? Not hours before, she had thought Mitch betrayed her. The euphoria of knowing she was finally free mingled with a weighty melancholy. Her horrific experience with Wade would always cast that shadow on her judgment, preventing her from committing herself to a good man, an excellent man, like Mitch.

She tried to force herself to celebrate. She could go anywhere, start over and work toward building her floral business, raise Ben, take that Disneyland trip. She'd shared all these plans with Nana Jo, who'd cried along with her. *Tomorrow*, she thought. *I'll leave tomorrow.* There would be one final night here at the ranch. Aunt Ginny and Uncle Gus had planned a quiet cookout.

She gathered Ben from his playtime and gave him another bath, as if she could wash away what had happened. She could only hope that Ben was young enough that other memories, the good memories she intended to make with him, would fill his heart to overflowing. With mixed emotions, she rocked Ben for the last time in the chair Mitch had provided.

Catty Cat followed them out to the campfire as the sun wilted into the horizon and darkness took its place. Lanterns strung across the patio danced spots of gold into the night sky, and the smell of grilling meats and a pot of chili in the kitchen perfumed the air.

Helen and Liam greeted her with smiles. Uncle Gus pressed a lemonade into her hand and a boxed juice for Ben. "Look who got invited to the cookout, Ben," Uncle Gus said.

Chad led Sugar up to the edge of the patio. The foal flicked her mane and whinnied, sending Ben into wide-eyed peals of delight.

"Would you like to pet her?" Uncle Gus said.

Ben nodded so hard he almost fell over. Uncle Gus and Chad led them onto the grass. Jane's vision went blurry as she watched her precious son, her gift from God, her solace and her joy.

"He doing okay?" Mitch said. He'd come close, thumbs hooked on his belt loops. Her stomach fluttered.

"Yes, he's okay," she said. "Thanks to you and your family."

"You did great before we got there," he said. They

lapsed into silence, strolling to the fence. It felt so right to be there with him, and so painful to consider that she'd leave the next day.

She pushed her hair behind her ears. "I'm sorry… that I didn't stay, that I didn't trust you."

He shook his head. "No need to say that."

"Yes, there is. Mitch, I didn't trust you, because I don't know how to trust. I think maybe I never will."

He turned her then, gently, and circled her wrists with his thumbs. "You just gotta have someone trustworthy around so you can practice on 'em."

She yearned for—no, craved—the chance to learn with Mitch, but she could not ask it of him. It was best for her to move on, and him, too. The sky grew suddenly darker, and Jane struggled to find even a single star.

Mitch was quiet, but she could sense that he was wrestling with what to say next. She was determined to be kind to him, to make their parting as easy as possible. "I think I'll go join Ben."

"Wait. I want to say something."

She stopped, trying to read his emotions, but the combination of lamplight and his stoic expression stymied her.

He rubbed a hand over his freshly shaven chin. "Do you know what my favorite time of year here at the ranch is?"

"Uh, no," she said, wondering why he felt the need to share such a topic.

He swallowed so hard she could hear the gulp. It ticked her pulse up a notch.

"Spring."

She nodded. "All the green grass and blue skies. I'm sure it's glorious."

"That's not why it's my favorite."

"Why, then?"

"Because the calves come, and they are new and full of wonder and…you make me feel like that."

"Mitch," she gasped. "I…I'm not sure what to say."

"Just listen," he said. "'Cause I've been practicing this in my mind so many times Liam is accusing me of having conversations with myself."

She put her fingers over her trembling lips and watched him suck in a deep breath. "When I'm with you, the world feels new and fresh and it makes me want to tear down the walls I've built up to keep the past out and start something new."

When he stopped speaking, she put her hand gently on his arm. "Mitch, I will treasure what you've said my whole life, but I've already told you, because of my past with Wade…" She forced herself to say it. "With your brother…"

"Wade has no ties on you anymore, and none on me, either. Remember what you said? Nothing can separate you from the love of God. I finally get what that means, because nothing, not the past or the pain or the troubles ahead or behind, is gonna make me love you any less. Only more—it's just gonna be more, every day, every year."

Every day, every year. What was he saying? What could she be hearing?

"I love you," he said, "and I love Ben, and that's the bare honest truth of it."

She thought it was the bravest thing she'd heard anyone say, ever, and it left her speechless.

"I think we could be a great family. Don't you?" He gazed at her, head slightly cocked, moonlight catching the planes of his face.

Out came the fear that held her captive. "I'm not sure how to be a wife to a good man."

He smiled shyly and took her hand, kissing the knuckles. "The same way I learned how to ride horses. The same way you learned how to be a spectacular mother to Ben—one step at a time, one day at a time."

"What if I fail?" she whispered.

"Do you trust me?" His eyes shone like black lightning. "Do you believe that I love you and I will take care of you and Ben every day for the rest of my life?"

Did she? Could she? He'd risked stepping through her walls and his, for her, for Ben. "Yes," she managed. "Yes, I do trust you."

Emotion rippled across his face. "And do you love me, Jane? Can you love me in spite of who I am and what my brother did to you?"

That one required no thought at all. She leaned forward and brushed her lips ever so gently against his, feeling his sigh. Love kicked up in her spirit, the love she'd been suppressing, caging, denying, bursting forth like a calf eager for the glorious feel of sunshine.

"I love you, Mitch. I…" He stepped close then and stopped her with a kiss.

"That's all I need to know, all I'll ever need to know." He lifted her off the ground.

"But wait… Mitch…how will we explain it to Ben? You're his uncle…but…"

"I'll be his uncle, his daddy, his coach and mentor or whatever he needs me to be. I'll raise him to know he's loved, no matter what he calls me, even if it's Moo Moo."

She cried then, too overcome to manage a word.

"And I'll build a house for the three of us here in Driftwood." His arms tightened around her as he put her down. "Unless… I mean…unless there are too many bad memories here."

She trailed her fingers along his face, skimming his cheeks, staring at him until the outline of the scar was no longer distinct from the other precious contours of his face. "Here," she whispered, letting the past fly away like the curls of smoke rising from the firepit. "Right here in Driftwood."

He laughed and pulled her close again, burying his face in her curls. She giggled and allowed him to whirl her around. Finally, at long last, she let herself accept that her life was about to begin anew, full of promise and the sweet taste of second chances. Tipping her face to the sky, she watched the moon rise over Roughwater Ranch, starting off on its path toward the ocean.

* * * * *

If you enjoyed this story, look for these other books by Dana Mentink from Love Inspired Suspense.

Cowboy Christmas Guardian
Treacherous Trails
Cowboy Bodyguard
Lost Christmas Memories

Dear Reader,

Miles of ocean, acres of grassland, plenty of heroes. Welcome to the Roughwater Ranch, owned by Aunt Ginny and Uncle Gus. I just adore a good cowboy story, don't you? In this series you'll meet Mitch, Liam, Helen and Chad, four people who are closer than kin, part of the glorious Roughwater Ranch family. All four books take place along the central California coast, a favorite spot of ours to visit. The last time we were there, we watched the sea lions hanging out on the beach, just across the road from herds of cattle grazing on the pastureland. Surf and turf at its finest! I hope you will enjoy coming along on my coastal cowboy adventures!

God bless and giddyup!
Dana Mentink

*With a bomber targeting New York City, two K-9 cops
will have to go undercover as a married couple to put
an end to an explosive crime spree.*

Read on for a sneak preview of
Deep Undercover *by Lenora Worth,*
the next exciting installment to the
True Blue K-9 Unit miniseries, available
July 2019 from Love Inspired Suspense.

K-9 officer Gavin Sutherland held tight to his K-9 partner
Tommy's leash and scanned the crowd, his mind on high
alert, his whole body tense as he tried to protect the city
he loved. People from all over the world stood shoulder
to shoulder along the East River, waiting for the annual
Fourth of July fireworks display.

His partner, a black-and-white springer spaniel, knew
the drill. Tommy worked bomb detection. He had been
trained to find incendiary devices. He knew to sniff the air
and the ground. Sniff, sit, repeat. Be rewarded.

Glancing up, Gavin spotted his backup, K-9 officer
Brianne Hayes, a rookie who had been paired with him to
continue gaining experience.

Brianne headed toward him, her auburn hair caught up
in a severe bun. That fire-colored hair matched her fierce
determination to prove herself since she was one of only a
few female K-9 officers in the city that never slept.

Brianne's partner, Stella, was also in training with the K-9 handlers.

"I've been along the perimeters of the park," Brianne said. "Nothing out of the ordinary. Can't wait for the show."

Scanning the area again, he said, "I think the crowd grows every year. Standing room only tonight."

"Stella keeps fidgeting and sniffing. She needs to get used to this."

Stella stopped and lifted her nose into the air, a soft growl emitting from her throat.

"Steady, girl. You'll need to contain that when the fireworks start."

But Stella didn't quit. The big dog tugged forward, her nose sniffing both air and ground.

Gavin watched the Labrador, wondering what kind of scent she'd picked up. Then Tommy alerted, going still except for his wagging tail that acted like a warning flag, his body trembling in place.

"Something's up," Gavin whispered to Brianne. "He's picked up a signature somewhere."

Brianne whispered low. "There's a bomb?"

Don't miss
Deep Undercover *by Lenora Worth,*
available July 2019 wherever
Love Inspired® Suspense *books and ebooks are sold.*

www.LoveInspired.com

Looking for inspiration in tales
of hope, faith and heartfelt romance?

Check out **Love Inspired**® and
Love Inspired® **Suspense** books!

New books available every month!

CONNECT WITH US AT:

Facebook.com/groups/HarlequinConnection

Facebook.com/HarlequinBooks

Twitter.com/HarlequinBooks

Instagram.com/HarlequinBooks

Pinterest.com/HarlequinBooks

ReaderService.com

Love Inspired®